It is Christmas Day at the Foundling Hospital and Hetty Feather receives an unexpected present. But Hetty's delight sparks jealousy, which soon turns to trouble, and dreaded Matron Bottomly is thrilled to exclude Hetty from the Christmas festivities.

Poor Hetty is distraught – but just when it seems that all is lost, a dear friend arrives to whisk her away for a Christmas like no other . . .

Full of friendship, fun and festive cheer, this is a perfect gift of a Christmas story.

HETTY FEATHER'S
CHRISTMAS

Jacqueline Wilson

HETTY FEATHER'S CHRISTMAS

Illustrated by NICK SHARRATT

DOUBLEDAY

DOUBLEDAY

UK | USA | Canada | Ireland | Australia
India | New Zealand | South Africa

Doubleday is part of the Penguin Random House group of companies
whose addresses can be found at global.penguinrandomhouse.com.

www.penguin.co.uk
www.puffin.co.uk
www.ladybird.co.uk

First published 2017

001

Text design by Becky Chilcott
Printed in Great Britain by Clays Ltd, St Ives plc

A CIP catalogue record for this book is available from the British Library

Hardback ISBN: 978–0–857–53553–5
International paperback ISBN: 978–0–857–53554–2

All correspondence to:
Doubleday
Penguin Random House Children's
80 Strand, London WC2R 0RL

MIX
Paper from
responsible sources
FSC
www.fsc.org   FSC® C018179

Penguin Random House is committed to a
sustainable future for our business, our readers
and our planet. This book is made from Forest
Stewardship Council® certified paper.

To Caroline

CONTENTS

FOREWORD

y name is Hetty Feather. I wonder if you've read my memoirs? I can't believe they've actually been published now. Imagine, all these grand folk reading the true story of a humble foundling girl! Though, if I'm truthful, I have never exactly acted humble. I always gave those fierce matrons at the Foundling Hospital a run for their money. And since my stage career I suppose I've become a little bit famous. If only Mama could see me now!

It must have been so terrible for her, having to put me in the care of the hospital. I was there for

nine bleak years, till I turned fourteen. I hated it there. We were all fed regular meals, but we were starved of love. We were all decently clothed in our identical brown uniforms, but we never knew the warmth of an embrace. It was such a monotonous life, day after day after day exactly the same, apart from chapel on Sundays and the gift of a penny and an orange every Christmas.

Except for one Christmas. Let me tell you about Christmas 1888, when I was twelve . . .

Hetty Feather

CHAPTER ONE

 woke up and immediately felt under my hard pillow, just in case I'd dreamed it. No, there it was – a small wrapped package that fitted neatly into the palm of my hand. I fingered the outline hidden inside the thick brown paper. It was hard to make sense of it. There was a triangle shape at one end, ridged in some kind of pattern. Then there were little bumps further down and a slightly bigger one in the middle. I couldn't work out what on earth it could be.

I tried to edge my finger inside the brown paper, but it had been tightly wrapped and tied into place

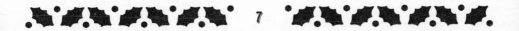

with string. I *could* just tear it off. I'd taken such a long time to fall asleep, tossing and turning, and slipping my hand under my pillow again and again, checking that my precious package was still there. But I'd slept eventually, probably for hours. It *must* be Christmas Day by now.

I so, so, so wanted to know what was in my parcel. But if I opened it now, I'd have nothing else to look forward to at Christmas. Somehow the waiting and the wondering were part of the whole joy of receiving a precious present.

One girl turned over in her narrow bed, murmuring something in her sleep. Several were breathing heavily, and someone was snoring like a pig. Sheila, definitely! I wished there was some way of waking her up so that she could listen to herself. She'd die of shame. She never believed it when I told her she snored. Her toadying friend Monica swore blind to Sheila that she didn't snore, though she slept right next to her and her entire bed rattled with the noise.

There were no sighs, no whispers, no muffled sobs. Everyone was fast asleep. I thought of all the other sleeping souls in the Foundling Hospital. My little foster sister, Eliza, was down the other end of the corridor with the other small girls. My foster brother, Gideon, was right over in the other wing with the big boys. I ached when I thought of him, near but so far away. My second foster brother, Saul, was even further off, lying still and snoreless in a grave behind the chapel. Or perhaps great wings had burst through his nightshirt and carried him aloft up to Heaven. I hoped so – though when he was alive and we were all living in the country cottage with our dear foster mother and father, I'd frequently wished he'd go to the devil.

I went hot with shame now, though it was a very cold night and my blanket was thin. Matron Bottomly would only allow us one blanket each, even when there was snow on the ground and the pipes froze solid. I had glimpsed her bed once when I was

called to her room. It had two big plump pillows and was piled high with quilts and blankets.

I pictured her now, lying on her back, her nightcap crooked, her mouth open and drooling. Perhaps she slept clasping her cane, ready, even in her dreams, to chastize any rebellious foundling. How I hated her! I'd always detested her, even more than Matron Pigface, who had ruled over us when we were new girls. When Matron Bottomly had banished Ida, my dearest mother, I hated her more than ever. It didn't seem sinful to wish that *she* would go to the devil. She was so heartlessly evil, even the devil himself would surely shun her company.

Then I heard the chapel clock ring out: *one, two, three*, clear in the crisp night air.

It was so cold! I tucked my icy feet up inside my nightgown and tried hugging myself. If only I had someone else to hug me. When I was little, I climbed in beside Jem. He would grumble, half asleep, and say I should go back to my own bed, but then his

strong arms would wrap themselves around me. He'd rub his chin on my wild red hair, and I felt so comforted I fell asleep in an instant.

After I discovered that Ida was my real mama, I stole away to her kitchen as often as I dared, and if we could be sure of being quite alone, she would sit on the bench and pat her lap, and I'd climb on and nestle there like a baby, even though I was growing up fast. I was still small and slight, though, and hopefully didn't squash Mama too much.

'You're light as a fairy, my little Hetty,' she'd murmur. 'I can't get enough cuddles with you. All those ten lonely years when I had to make do without any opportunity. Oh, it was *so* hard.'

It's even harder now, because I know she's my mother and we love each other so much. She would still be working in the kitchen at the Foundling Hospital if it wasn't for Sheila spying on us, and Matron Bottomly sending Mama packing. She said she was wicked and deceitful, and when Mama cried

out that she'd only lied because she loved me so and needed to be near me, Matron Bottomly called her a fallen woman who had no right to her child because I'd been born in sin.

'All right, punish *me* if you must – but why deny Hetty a mother's love? She's just an innocent child. She can't help being born out of wedlock,' Mama protested bravely.

'Hetty Feather is a red-haired child of Satan, a wilful imp who needs to be shamed and tamed,' Matron Bottomly said.

Well, she's done enough shaming and taming me these past eighteen months to last me a lifetime, but I have a fiery spirit to match my fiery hair and she'll never, ever, ever change the way I feel.

She'll never change Mama, either. She has to work as a maid hundreds of miles away and we can't see each other any more, but Miss Smith acts as our secret postman. Mama sends short letters because writing doesn't come easily to her, but even if the

 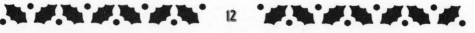

messages are brief – *Deerest Hetty, I love love love you and miss you horibbly your own Mama* – they are more beautiful to me than any Shakespearean sonnet.

I've kept every letter, folding them again and again and tying them with ribbon. I roll the sweetest messages up in tiny spills and post them into my pillow. I imagine them whispering words of love in my ears as I sleep.

I write long letters back, printing in big letters so that Mama can read each word easily. Miss Smith gives me notepaper, but sometimes I run out and have to tear pages out of my journal. Miss Smith bought that for me too. She has been such a dear friend to me, a true fairy godmother.

I couldn't help smiling into the darkness at the thought of Miss Smith dressed in flouncy taffeta, with wings and a wand. In reality, she is a stout, white-haired lady with a long horse's face. However much I care about her, I could never call her pretty

or even handsome. But she is good and kind and she has been so, so generous to me.

Now that she has become a governor of the Foundling Hospital, I see her quite often. She paid a special visit yesterday, Christmas Eve, accompanied by a sturdy lad carrying a great trunk that rattled deafeningly. They had been to the bank to collect the Christmas pennies for all the foundlings. She left the lad recovering in the kitchen with a glass of something strong and said she might as well make a quick inspection of the premises while she was here.

I'm sure that request set Matron Bottomly all a-quiver. Years ago we older foundlings had discovered that she sells off half the food and most of the wool and linen sent to feed and clothe us. I dare say she'd like to get her hands on our coppers too.

She steered Miss Smith around cautiously, glaring at us all as we darned, sighing over our socks.

'It's practical for the girls to learn to darn neatly,

but it's such repetitive work,' Miss Smith said. 'Perhaps we could leave the darning to the little ones, and see if the older girls can tackle some proper sewing. If I had some fine linen and white embroidery silks sent to the hospital, they could make themselves some attractive undergarments.'

Our heads jerked up in surprise, and there were several pricked fingers. We'd never, ever been given *under*garments! Our stiff brown frocks chafed against our bare skin. We barely knew what undergarments looked like, though I had a dim memory of my older foster sisters dancing about the moonlit bedroom in their white chemises and lace-trimmed drawers.

'That's a very interesting idea, Miss Smith, but embroidered undergarments would not be appropriate for our girls,' said Matron Bottomly, tight-lipped. 'They are being trained for service.'

'Well, I will bring the matter up at the next board meeting,' said Miss Smith smoothly. 'Now, let me

inspect these socks. Dear me, some seem to be more darns than wool!'

She wandered around, peering at each girl's work. When Matron Bottomly tutted over Slow Freda's huge stitches, Miss Smith took the small brown parcel out of her carpet bag and dropped it in my lap.

'From Ida!' she mouthed.

I had tucked it down the front of my dress in an instant. There was plenty of room as I still have no chest to speak of, though a few of the girls my age are starting to look quite womanly. Sheila is as flat as me, but when we go to chapel on a Sunday and parade past the boys, she looks quite shapely. She wears her socks rolled up inside her dress instead of on her feet!

For the rest of the day I walked with my stomach sticking out so that the precious parcel wouldn't work its way down and shoot right out from under my skirts. While we were saying our prayers at

bedtime, I hid it under my pillow in a flash – and here it was now, tight in my hand.

I thought of Mama's hands carefully wrapping it in the paper and tying it with string. I mimed the motions, picturing it so vividly it was almost like holding her real work-worn hands and small nimble fingers. I thought of all the time we could have spent together but had been denied. I still had another two wretched years at the Foundling Hospital before it was time for me to leave, and even then I wouldn't be free to find her. All foundling girls had to seek employment as servants, living in someone else's house, at their beck and call from dawn till dusk.

I could only hope that Miss Smith might find me a position near Mama so that we might see each other for a stolen hour or two each week. It needn't be in the same town. I would walk ten miles to see my mama, even twenty. I would walk until my feet were one big blister so long as I could

have five minutes in her arms.

The longing for her was so strong that I had to close my eyes tight to stop my tears rolling sideways and dampening my pillow. I turned on my side, parcel held as carefully as a rescued fledgling, and tried hard to get back to sleep. I sang inside my head to soothe myself.

All week we'd been practising Christmas carols for today's service in the chapel. I worked my way through the repertoire, thinking of all those mild mothers and blessed infants in their lowly stable refuge, turned away by decent folk. All the foundlings had been born in similar secret circumstances. Our mothers probably loved us just as much as Mary loved the infant Jesus. Certainly Mama had loved me like that. But she couldn't find a job where she was allowed to keep me with her, and she had no husband to support us. She *had* to give me up. We'd all been handed in to the hospital and our mothers had stumbled away weeping while, in Matron's

cold arms, we bawled too. I hoped I'd wet right through my napkin and stained her starched white apron.

I fell asleep at last and dreamed I was a baby again, lying in Mama's arms, and Three Wise Women came to give me gifts. My foster mother, Peg, gave me a rag baby, Madame Adeline from the travelling circus gave me a tiny pink spangled dress, and Miss Smith gave me a leather notebook in which to write my future memoirs.

They all sang to me, but their voices were harsh and high-pitched and grew louder and louder – and I woke to the jangling of the morning bell.

'Wake up, girls!' the morning monitor shouted.

She wished each girl a merry Christmas as she paused to light our candle stubs so we could see to get dressed. There were groans and yawns and sleepy responses. I drew the blanket high over my head, leaving a little gap so that I could just about see by the flickering candle, then pulled off the

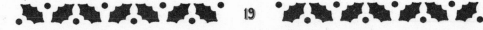

parcel string and wound it tight around my wrist like a bracelet. Then I carefully unpeeled the brown paper, trying hard not to let it crackle. I came upon a little note folded small between the layers. I held the blanket higher, straining to read it.

> Deer Hetty
> Merry merry merry Crismass darling child. I am saving and saving and one day we wil live in a litel hous like this.
> With all my love
> Mama

I clutched the letter in shaking hands and then kissed the word *Mama* thirteen times – a kiss for every year of my life, and one extra for luck. Then I unwrapped the final piece of brown paper and gaped in wonder.

I was holding a little house – a perfect tiny house made out of driftwood, with a tiled roof fashioned

from minute shells. They were painted red, and the walls of the house carefully whitewashed. There were three windows outlined in green, with tiny scraps of curtain at each: matching blue gingham at the top two, red velvet at the lower one. The door was painted dark green, with a sliver of yellow stone as a door knocker.

Our little house, Mama's and mine. I couldn't hold back my tears.

'What are you doing under there, Hetty Feather?' Sheila demanded, and pulled my blanket off before I could stop her.

'She's crying!' Monica jeered.

'No I'm not!' I said furiously, sniffing hard. I tried to hide the little house under my pillow but I wasn't quick enough.

'What's that?' Sheila demanded.

'Nothing! Get off!' I said, trying to grab her hand, but she got there first.

'Whatever's this?' she said, holding it aloft so

that the whole dormitory could gawp at my precious present. 'It's a little toy! Hetty's got a baby toy!'

I sprang at her, pulling her hair and seizing her wrist.

'Ow! Stop it, you're hurting!' Sheila screamed.

'Give it back or I'll pull your hair right out of your head,' I threatened, and I tried to snatch my house back.

Sheila clung onto it and we struggled.

One of the tiny shell tiles flew off the roof and fell on the floor.

'Now look! Oh, the *roof*!' I said desperately.

'*You* did it!' said Sheila, but she let go of the house.

I cradled it in my hand, bending to pick up the little shell. 'You've spoiled it,' I said.

'Don't be so silly – you can easily glue it back on,' she told me.

'Where did you get it from, Hetty?' asked Monica. 'Did you steal it?'

'It's mine! It's a Christmas present from Mama,'

I said. 'There! See how precious it is.'

The others gathered around, peering at it.

'Is it really from your mama?' Freda asked. Her voice wobbled when she said the word.

'Yes, it is! None of *you* have Christmas presents from your mothers,' I said.

There was a sudden silence. It was a word we seldom used. It brought back too many painful memories. We'd all lost our own real mothers, and then, when we were five and returned to the hospital, we'd also lost our foster mothers.

'Oh, Hetty, you're so lucky!' said Freda, and the others echoed her.

Even Monica looked wistful and gazed at the little house in awe. 'It's wonderful, Hetty,' she whispered.

Sheila's face darkened. 'I don't know why you're all making such a fuss. It's just a silly home-made toy. A baby house made out of scraps. It's not wonderful at all.'

'It *is*! My mama made it specially for me,' I said

proudly. 'It must have taken her ages and ages. It shows just how much she loves me.'

'Your mama's only *Ida*,' said Sheila, her face contorted. 'She was a kitchen maid. It's not as if she's anyone special.'

I gasped and then flew at her. I hit out blindly with both fists, so desperate to defend my dear mama that I didn't pause to think what I was doing.

I was still holding the little house in my hand!

The house glanced off Sheila's forehead, the shells scratching her, and then it jerked out of my hand onto the floor. It landed with a terrible thump. More shells flew off, and the walls came apart. My little house was ruined!

CHAPTER TWO

 hate you, I hate you!' I cried, kneeling on the floor and sweeping up the little shells with trembling fingers. The girls gathered around me, stunned.

'Poor Hetty,' said one.

'Oh, Sheila, you shouldn't have spoiled her little house,' said Freda.

'*I* didn't do it! *She* did it! And look – she's really hurt me, I'm bleeding!' said Sheila, dabbing at the scratch on her forehead. She bent over me. 'You came at me like a lunatic! You're going to end up in Bedlam, Hetty Feather!'

'You're enough to drive anyone crazy. How *could* you! *Look!*' I held up the poor battered house. 'I'll never be able to mend it. It's all lopsided now.'

'It was lopsided in the first place. It was just a little gimcrack toy. A child of six would have sneered at it. I don't know why you're making such a fuss. If *my* mother gave me a doll's house, it would be as big as me, with proper rooms inside, and lots of china dolls, not a useless little matchbox,' said Sheila.

I tugged at the hem of her nightgown, jerking her off her feet, and then we were both rolling around the dormitory floor, hitting out and spitting. I was in such a rage I could see red mist before my eyes, but I suddenly became aware that there was a silence. Sheila wriggled away from me, sobbing. I blinked. I saw big stout black boots, black lisle stockings and the crisp hem of apron.

Matron Bottomly!

She seized me by the scruff of the neck and

pulled me up. 'Hetty Feather! Trust you to be the girl behaving like a savage animal on Our Lord's birthday!' she hissed. 'Look at the state of poor Sheila!'

'She asked for it,' I said through gritted teeth.

'She hurt me,' Sheila sobbed, dabbing at her forehead with her sleeve. There was only a little smear of blood, but she was making so much fuss you'd have thought she was gushing like a fountain.

'I will *not* have this behaviour, especially on such a holy day,' said Matron Bottomly. 'You will go without breakfast, Hetty Feather. And if you misbehave again in any way whatsoever, you will forfeit your Christmas lunch into the bargain. Now stop gawping and get dressed, all of you.'

She turned – and one of her stout boots kicked my little house. 'What's this rubbish?' she said, peering down. Then she lifted her foot and stamped down hard on the house, utterly flattening it.

I screamed.

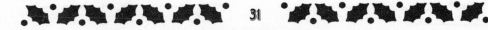 

'Stop that noise and get it cleared up at once!' she said.

'It's not rubbish, you wicked, evil woman! It's my house and you've deliberately smashed it, and now I'll never, ever be able to mend it!' I cried, and I stamped hard on her horrible boots in retaliation.

The girls gasped. Even Sheila stopped bleating.

'How *dare* you!' Matron Bottomly shook first one foot, then the other. 'My Lord, you could have broken my toes! I'm not standing for this, Hetty Feather. I gave you a chance. Now you will be severely punished.'

She seized me by the hair and hauled me towards the door. I struggled, but it hurt so badly when I tried to pull away that I had to follow.

'Oh, Matron, it wasn't really Hetty's fault!' Freda cried out. 'She was just upset because—'

'No, Freda! Don't say any more!' I interrupted desperately. If Matron Bottomly found out that

 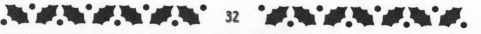

Miss Smith had been our postman, she'd never let me see her again.

Matron Bottomly glared at Freda. 'Come on then, girl! What were you going to say?' she demanded.

Freda bit her lip. 'I forget,' she quavered. She looked at Sheila, who went red in the face but stayed silent.

I was dragged out of the dormitory, all the way along the corridor. I was so distraught at the loss of Mama's little house that I was almost past caring. But when Matron started pulling me up the narrow staircase to the attic, I started struggling.

'Please, Matron, don't lock me up in that punishment cupboard! Please, please, please! I shall die if you lock me in there again!' I begged.

'You should have thought of that when you attacked me!' she said, panting with the effort of dragging me along. 'You will have time to think of the consequences of your wickedness when you are alone up here.'

'But it's Christmas Day!'

'Yes, it is, and you will miss all the wonderful treats,' she said.

I didn't care about my penny or the orange we were given for lunch, but I'd been looking forward to seeing the Christmas tableau in the chapel for months.

It was always a glorious sight: the head girl clothed in bright blue with a white veil about her head, instead of her brown frock and mob cap, the three tall lads decked out in brocade, with gilt crowns and false beards, and the little ones trying so hard to keep as still as statues as they tended their toy sheep. But I only had eyes for the Angel Gabriel, suspended on ropes high above our head, because it had become a tradition that he was played by my brother Gideon. I barely caught a glimpse of him all year because the boys were kept quite separate from us, even using the recreation area at different times, and if we tried to peer over into their half of the chapel on Sundays, we got severely rapped

about the head by a watchful nurse.

But during the Christmas service, for a full hour or more, I could stare up at Gideon, my head craned backwards until it ached. I was never sure whether he could see me or not. I was probably an indistinguishable blur amongst a mass of mob caps, but I liked to fancy that he was looking down at me – maybe that was why he was smiling so radiantly, the red and yellow and blue light from the stained-glass window reflecting on his white gown.

At the thought of him looking around in vain for a glimpse of bright red hair beneath a cap I started to cry.

'Yes, well might you cry, Hetty Feather,' said Matron, pulling me harder, her strength suddenly renewed as we neared the dreadful punishment room.

I wailed even harder at the sight of that strong door and the large key in the lock. I could batter myself against it until I knocked myself senseless but I could never escape.

Matron Bottomly paused, both hands on my shoulders now, her strong fingers digging into my flesh. 'Are you sorry now, Hetty Feather?' she demanded.

Was she offering me one last chance? I threw all notions of pride away. I would endure anything rather than be imprisoned there all day, and likely all night long as well.

'Yes, I'm truly sorry, Matron! Sorry from the bottom of my heart! I won't ever be so wicked again! I shall do my best to repent all my sins. Please find it in your good heart to forgive me,' I cried.

Matron Bottomly's fingers loosened just a fraction. She looked at me closely. Then her face smoothed out. 'It's Christmas Day, a day for rejoicing at the birth of Our Lord. A day to remind us that little Lord Jesus loves us all and forgives us when we have sinned. So I *do* forgive you, Hetty Feather,' she said, emphasizing each word as if reading the sermon in the pulpit.

My whole body went limp with relief. I would have fallen on the floor if she hadn't been holding me tightly. 'Thank you, Matron,' I whispered.

I saw the gleam in her eyes. A crooked smile distorted her face. She grabbed my hair again, right at the roots so I couldn't twist and turn, and reached for the key.

'In you go!' she said, whipping the door open and thrusting me inside.

'No! I said sorry! You said you forgave me!' I screamed.

'I do indeed forgive you, Hetty Feather, because I am a Christian woman who practises what she preaches, but that doesn't mean I am weak and foolish. I've always believed in "Spare the rod and spoil the child". You must still be punished. I would be failing in my duties if I let you off now. What sort of example would it be to your sister foundlings?' She gave me one last shove and I landed on my bottom in the tiny dank room.

'You don't really forgive me!' I screamed. 'You were just tormenting me! You hate me as much as I hate you! I'm glad I stamped on your feet. I wish I'd stamped on the rest of you as well!'

I went on screaming abuse at her long after the door had clanged shut. I screamed until my throat was sore. I hurled myself at the door, even though I knew it was pointless. Then I curled up in a corner, my hands over my head.

When I was locked in the punishment room the first time, Mama had risked everything and come to find me. She couldn't set me free because Matron had taken away the key, but she had knelt on the other side of the door and whispered to me for hours. It was such a comfort. I didn't know she was my mama then – she was simply Ida – but I loved her because she had always been so kind to me. She'd helped me imagine that I was lying on a soft bed with a warm blanket over me – she'd made it seem so real.

I tried picturing for myself, but I couldn't manage

it now. I was lying on a cold hard floor, and now that my temper had died down I was shivering violently, utterly freezing. My stomach rumbled angrily too. I thought of all the foundlings having their Christmas breakfast, with a teaspoon of sugar on their porridge as a treat. I had nothing to eat, nothing to drink. Last time I'd been given only bread and water. I wasn't sure I'd even get that now. There was an old tin bucket in one corner so that I could relieve myself – this was their only provision.

'Oh, Mama,' I whispered, and my tears dripped down my face.

I knuckled my eyes and found I had a little chip of something stuck under my fingernail. I realized that it was a curved edge of shell from the roof of the little house. I stroked it against my cheek, imagining Mama getting up very early and creeping down to the sea-shore before making her mistress's breakfast. She'd gather pieces of driftwood and tiny shells and slivers of glass worn smooth by the sea

and then thrust them deep in her apron pocket. They'd clink softly against each other all day, and then, late at night, when the old lady was fast asleep, Mama would sit cross-legged by candlelight and start assembling my house.

It must have taken her so many days – and now it was smashed for ever.

'I'm so sorry, Mama,' I wept.

She'd be up now, maybe humming a Christmas carol as she boiled an egg for her mistress, smiling at the thought of me opening my parcel. I felt such an ache inside me, a pain that was nothing to do with hunger. I'd loved my foster mother, Peg, but nowhere near as much as my own mama.

It didn't do to think of Peg, either – or my first five Christmases in that cottage in the country. We were poor and often had to make do with bread and dripping and bacon scraps, but on Christmas Day we ate like kings. The farmer always sent us a goose, and Peg roasted it until the whole cottage smelled

heavenly and was as warm as summer. We decked the big room downstairs with sprays of holly and hanging ivy, and the older girls fashioned clumps of mistletoe into balls and hung them from the ceiling, hoping that some of the young farmhands might come calling.

The younger ones had kisses under the mistletoe too – the boys from Peg and the girls from my foster father, John. I kissed my foster brothers as well – big Ned and sly Saul and sweet Gideon. When it came to Jem, I was shameless, demanding so many kisses he joked that I was wearing out his lips.

I'd loved Jem so. In our special squirrel house he had patiently played all my games, listened to my silly stories, taught me to climb and catch and read and write, and then, when the amazing Tanglefield's Travelling Circus came to the village, he'd managed to sneak us in under the tent flap so that I could see the show.

When I closed my eyes and pictured my country

childhood, I saw all the soft greens and browns of nature, but the trip to the circus dazzled with the scarlet of the ringmaster's coat, the orange and purple of the clowns and, above all else, the pink sparkles of Madame Adeline, who rode her six rosin-backed horses so splendidly.

For years I'd been convinced that Madame Adeline was my real mother, simply because we both had bright red hair. When, much later, on the day of Queen Victoria's Golden Jubilee, I met her again, I realized that she was an old lady and her red hair a wig.

I wished now that she'd let me join the circus too! I'd wear a spangled dress and ride the horses in the ring, and have pink and yellow marzipan cake every night for supper.

Oh, how I loved cake! I especially loved it when Miss Smith took me for special outings to London teashops. Last time she'd taken me to the Northgate Tearooms in Piccadilly, along with Clover, a girl

who'd just arrived at her Home for Destitute Girls.
I thought Clover would mock my hideous brown
uniform and comical cap – after all, Miss Smith's
girls wear beautiful soft blue dresses without
any kind of hat. But she was shy and sweet, and
by the time we'd eaten our enormous tea we were
firm friends.

I thought of the rose sponge cakes and the coffee-
iced éclairs and the meringues and the lemon tarts
and the cherry pie and the chocolate gateau and
the pink and white and yellow buns. My empty
stomach growled.

When I was small, I could picture things so
vividly that they became real for me. I tried so hard
now to taste the sweet richness of the cakes on my
tongue. I struggled to inhale their scent of sugar and
rose and lemon and chocolate. I cupped my hands to
feel their softness and stickiness.

I couldn't make it work. My tongue was dry in
my mouth, my nose smelled stale air, my hands

stayed empty. None of my senses would work – except my ears. I heard a soft pattering, getting nearer. Someone was creeping along the corridor towards me.

My heart thumped hard in my chest. Was Matron Bottomly coming back for me after all? But she walked with firm steps – *stomp stomp, stomp stomp*. This was a lighter tread. Perhaps she'd sent one of the girls to set me free . . . I was in such a wretched state that I was willing to believe anything, although I knew that Matron Bottomly would never, ever relent. *Her* chest was an empty cavern, without any heart at all.

'Hetty?' There was a tiny whisper outside the door. 'Oh, Hetty, are you in there?' It sounded small and very frightened.

I knew that little piping voice. 'Eliza?' I whispered back.

'Oh, Hetty, yes, it's me! Your little sister!'

Eliza had been a baby when Peg took Gideon and

me back to the Foundling Hospital. It had been such a delightful surprise when, five years later, she'd arrived at the hospital herself. At first we'd been very close, but then she'd unwittingly dashed all my hopes for a future with dear Jem. She'd claimed that he was *her* true love – when she was older, he was going to take *her* away and make *her* his own little wife.

This had been *my* dream, *my* hope – though I can now see that it was just a childish fantasy. I'd been mean to Eliza – I couldn't bear her prattling away about 'her' Jem all the time. I'd brushed her aside, always too busy to play with her. Eventually she'd stopped trailing after me and had made friends with the other little ones. Yet now here she was, creeping up forbidden stairs and along dark corridors, just to find me!

'Oh, Eliza!' I said, my voice wobbling.

'Don't cry, Hetty! Try to be brave. I'm sure they'll let you out soon,' she insisted.

'But how did you know I was locked up here?'

'I looked for you at breakfast. I have a Christmas present for you! I asked the girls in your dormitory and they said you were being punished. It's so unfair! So I thought I'd find you and wish you a merry Christmas.'

'Oh bless you, darling. Well, Merry Christmas to you too. But you must run back quickly. They'll be going into chapel soon and your nurse will see that you're missing. You don't want to end up being punished.'

'But I had to make sure you were all right,' Eliza persisted. 'There's a little crack under your door. Perhaps I can pass your present underneath . . .'

There was a sudden thumping sound.

'What are you doing, Eliza?' I asked anxiously.

'I'm stamping on your present so it can go through the crack,' she said.

'Oh, don't!' I cried, seeing Matron's boot stamping on the little house all over again.

'It's all right. I won't hurt it. It's wrapped up

anyway. It's a little slab of toffee. One of the visitor ladies gave it to me last Sunday. I thought it would make a special Christmas present for you. I just opened it up and had a tiny lick. I hope you don't mind,' she said.

'Oh, Eliza. No, you must keep it for yourself,' I said, but she was already posting it through to me.

'It's yours, Hetty. Merry Christmas!' she squeaked, and then scuttled off down the corridor.

I picked up the flat, sticky parcel and then I ate the toffee. It tasted wonderful, even though the paper had stuck to it and it was a little fluffy in places. I felt cheered again, loving my dear, funny little sister.

CHAPTER
THREE

made my last bit of toffee last as long as I could, trying to coat my tongue with it so that the taste would stay with me. Every minute in that locked room was like an hour or more. After a while I dozed, and woke with a crick in my neck and a raging thirst that was even worse than my hunger.

I heard the chapel bells and I realized that they were only just filing in for the Christmas morning service – it already seemed like the middle of the afternoon. I passed the time conducting my own service, singing every carol I could remember in

spite of my dry throat. I asked God to bless all the people I loved most. I'm afraid I suggested He might curse Matron Bottomly and Sheila while He was at it.

After chapel everyone would file into the great dining hall for their Christmas meal. No boiled mutton – roast goose today! I swallowed hard, trying to ease my parched throat, remembering the Christmas mug of ginger beer. And, best of all, the plum pudding!

When Mama was working at the Foundling Hospital, I had helped her stir those huge bowls of pudding mixture. I tried so hard to be of use, but after only five minutes my arm ached terribly. Mama laughed and rolled up her sleeves to show me the big strong muscles in her slender arms.

When I slept again, I dreamed of her, and it seemed like a dream sent straight from Heaven to soothe me, because Mama and I were living together in our little house by the sea. Gulls perched on our shell-

tiled roof and salty breezes flapped our gingham curtains. We went for walks along the beach hand in hand, bought some fresh cod from a fisherman by the harbour, and then went home to fry it for our tea. But it grew dark and stormy and the little house shook in the strong winds. We heard the shells smashing on the ground, and then suddenly the whole roof was ripped off.

I clung to Mama, but I couldn't hold on tightly enough. She was whirled away from me, high up into the black sky. I tried to leap up after her, but the wooden walls fell on top of me, pinning me to the floor. I banged on the wood, desperate to get out, banging, banging, banging . . .

'Let me out!' I cried, waking myself up.

'I'm coming, Hetty! I'm here!' a voice called, and then I heard the sound of a key turning in the lock.

The door opened and I blinked in the sudden light. I saw a tall figure in an old-fashioned black silk dress, with a bonnet framing her long pale face.

'Miss Smith!' I gasped.

'You poor child!' she said, grabbing my hands and helping me out into the corridor.

I threw my arms around her waist and hugged her tightly. She stiffened at first because she was such a dignified lady, but then her arms went round me in return.

'There, there, my dear. You're safe now. I will make sure that you are never, ever punished in this barbaric way again,' she murmured.

I peered round her silky bulk. Matron Bottomly was standing in the corridor, arms folded, face grim.

'I appreciate your concern, Miss Smith,' she said, her voice oily and cloying. 'It pains me to punish any of my little charges in this way. But I am afraid Hetty Feather has sinned so gravely that I'm sure all the other governors would insist she be taught a lesson. She attacked me most brutally, ma'am, deliberately stamping on me, and savaged one of the other children very badly, drawing blood. What else

was I to do? I have to protect my girls and my staff. In any other establishment she would have received a good beating – but pray examine her, ma'am. You will not find a mark on her.'

'I will *not* examine her. I don't agree with treating little girls like horseflesh! Neither do I feel that incarcerating them like convicted criminals is a suitable way to help them see the error of their ways. At my own Home for Destitute Girls I find that children respond to kindness and reason,' said Miss Smith. She spoke very calmly but I could feel her trembling with indignation.

'I dare say you have your ways, ma'am, and I have mine,' said Matron Bottomly. 'Might I point out that you are a very new governor and unused to our methods. I have been employed here for more than twenty years and I have never had one complaint. I think you will find that the rest of the Board of Governors are entirely satisfied with my regime here.'

'That may be so,' said Miss Smith. 'They are mostly elderly military gentleman who know nothing about little children. But let us stop our pointless discussion – I can see we are never going to agree.' She turned to me, holding me gently at arm's length. 'I think you need to wash and dress yourself, Hetty, before I take you out.'

Take me out?!

Matron Bottomly looked astonished. 'Take her out?' she queried.

'I have been given permission by the Board of Governors to take a foundling child for an outing at any time I see fit,' said Miss Smith. 'As I'm sure you're aware, Matron Bottomly.'

'But it's Christmas Day, Miss Smith!'

'Exactly. And as it is now gone two o'clock, it is obvious that Hetty has missed her Christmas dinner. I will therefore make sure she has a festive tea. I will return her long before her bedtime. Now come along, Hetty,' she said, holding out her hand.

I took it, squeezing her mittened fingers. As we marched past Matron Bottomly, I couldn't help giving her a triumphant nod. Matron's eyes narrowed. I knew she'd punish me for it later but I didn't care. Miss Smith was my saviour! I was free.

I hurriedly splashed my tear-stained face with cold water, pulled off my nightgown and dressed in my brown uniform, with a clean cap, apron and tippet. I dragged a brush through my wild hair and even tried to polish my old boots by rubbing them on the backs of my legs. I presented myself to Miss Smith with a little curtsy.

'That's better, dear. Come along,' she said. 'Where's your coat?'

'I don't have one, Miss Smith. We sometimes put old sacks round our shoulders if it's really bitterly cold,' I explained.

'Old sacks!' said Miss Smith, sniffing. 'I can see the Board of Governors needs to be dragged into the nineteenth century. Come here, dear.'

She wrapped her own thick black cashmere shawl around me and hurried me along. It was so strange to go down the main stairs, step across the chequered floor of the hallway and out through the big oak door. We went down the long promenade walk to where Miss Smith's carriage was waiting. I couldn't help skipping, though my ankles kept turning over because my boots were too big for me.

Miss Smith smiled at me but then shook her head. 'I don't know why I'm smiling, Hetty. Whatever possessed you to attack one of the other foundlings?'

'I thought you'd be crosser about my attacking Matron Bottomly,' I said.

'Not at all. I frequently feel like attacking her myself!' said Miss Smith. 'At board meetings I've tried to suggest she's not caring enough, but those old fogeys think she's doing a splendid job. After Christmas I shall report to them and say she locked you up when she'd promised not to employ that form

of punishment again, but I know they'll only give her the mildest of reprimands. Just think, I gave that dreadful woman a bottle of the finest sherry to share with the staff for Christmas. I hope it chokes her!'

'It's so marvellous that you see right through her, Miss Smith,' I said. 'And even more marvellous that you've rescued me!'

'And I intend to do my best to make up for your incarceration and lost Christmas dinner! But you still haven't told me why you attacked a fellow foundling and drew blood. That sounds very savage!' said Miss Smith. 'I hope Matron Bottomly was exaggerating.'

'I think it *was* a savage attack, but she hardly bled at all – it was just a little scratch and it was really all her fault. She insulted my mama and her wonderful present. It was the most perfect little house made out of seashells and driftwood . . . and now it's smashed to smithereens . . .' I said, and my voice quavered.

'Poor Hetty,' said Miss Smith, and she put her arm round me consolingly. 'Though you're a very naughty girl to reciprocate so violently.'

'Well, she's so hateful, Miss Smith!' I protested.

'That's no excuse. And have you never wondered *why* she behaves hatefully? Perhaps she envies you, and wishes with all her heart that *she* was in touch with her real mother,' said Miss Smith as we reached her carriage.

I thought about it as her driver, Albert, bowed solemnly as if I was a real lady, handed me up the steps and onto the leather seat. Miss Smith sat down beside me, her voluminous black silk skirts covering me like a slippery rug.

I turned to her. 'Perhaps you're right,' I said reluctantly. 'You have a clever way of making me think, Miss Smith. If I could only be a student at your Home for Destitute Girls, I'm sure I would learn to be as good as gold. Don't I qualify as *destitute*? Couldn't you possibly take me in?'

'I wish I could, my dear, but you are legally the charge of the Foundling Hospital. Still, take heart. You have only two more years, and then I hope to find an excellent position for you, and in the fullness of time I'm sure you and your mother will be able to be together. Now, let us make the most of today. You need to be fed!'

'Might we be going to the Northgate Tearooms?' I exclaimed.

'No, I think they will be closed for Christmas. I am relying on you to eat heartily, Hetty. I am already uncomfortably full. I ate a Christmas breakfast with the girls at my home, and then had goose and plum pudding with the matrons and the other governors here at the hospital. Matron Bottomly didn't breathe a word about your punishment, but luckily, when I was about to leave, one of the little girls plucked at my skirt and whispered that her sister had been locked in the attic.'

'Oh, that's little Eliza. She came to find me. Bless

her!' I said. 'Could she come on one of our outings someday, Miss Smith?'

'Of course she can. She seems a dear little soul,' she replied.

'So where are we going now, Miss Smith? Are we having tea at your house?'

'I think you would find that very disappointing. I've let my cook go to her own family this Christmas so I'd only be able to rustle up a plate of bread and butter,' she said.

'I'm sure that would be delicious,' I declared politely, which made her laugh again.

'We're going to have tea with a very dear friend and colleague of mine, Mr Edward Rivers. I haven't met his family yet but I'm sure they will make you very welcome, Hetty. Mr Rivers is an artist. He illustrates my books, and very splendidly too,' said Miss Smith.

'If you were to write a story about the Foundling Hospital, would he draw me? Oh, please, Miss Smith,

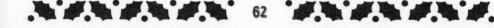

do write a story about us! Think what fun you would have portraying Matron Bottomly! You could have her doing such outrageous things, but then she would get her comeuppance, outwitted by a little red-haired foundling girl!' I said enthusiastically.

'Perhaps *you* can write that story one day, dear. I don't think I'd last long as a governor if I wrote such a thing – and if I *am* a governor, I can use what little influence I have to try to improve the lot of all you girls and boys.'

'Well, you've certainly improved my lot today! So your friend is an artist, Miss Smith? I once read a tale about an artist in Cook's *Police Gazette*, but he was starving in a garret. Are all artists very poor?' Perhaps it would be bread and butter after all, which was a vast improvement on no food at all, but not as exciting as the prospect of cake.

'This gentleman is very comfortably off, and I believe his wife comes from a wealthy family too. They live in a delightful four-storey house in Kensington.'

'Four storeys for just two people?' I was astonished.

'No, no, they have a big family – six or seven children – and staff as well, of course. One of my girls recently took up a position there. I think you'll be pleased when you see who it is.'

'I shall be staff one day,' I said, not concentrating. 'I wish I didn't have to be. I shall work hard on my memoirs and make my fortune when they're published. Then I'll become a proper lady like you, with a fine carriage like this, and I'll wear long silk dresses too – but I think mine will be green because that would look good with my red hair – and *I* will have a delightful four-storey house in Kensington, wherever that is, and Mama and I will live there together. We will have a room to sit in and a room to sleep in and a room to cook in and a room to eat in and a room for all our dresses and a room for all our books and a room for dancing in and a room for singing in and a room for writing in and – and—'

'And a room for resting quietly in!' said Miss

Smith. 'My goodness, Hetty, you've scarcely drawn breath for the last ten minutes. Calm down, child.'

'My foster mother, Peg, used to say that I was like a little woodpecker, going *peck, peck, peck* at her. I can't help it, Miss Smith! At the hospital we have to be silent most of the time, so now I'm out I just want to talk and talk!' I peered out of the carriage window. 'Where are we now? Might this be Hampstead? I went there on the day of the Queen's Golden Jubilee.'

'No, no, we're going in quite the other direction.'

'Are we going as far as the sea? Oh, Miss Smith, is Kensington near Bignor, where Mama is? It would be so wonderful to see her, even if it's just to wish her Merry Christmas and give her a hug.'

'I wish with all my heart that it was possible, Hetty dear, but the seaside is much further away. We would have to travel all day to reach it. I'd never be able to get you back to the hospital in time,' she said.

'Well, that would be a bonus!' I said. 'I could stay overnight. You could pretend I'd been captured by

a gang of brigands again. Do you remember you did that when I ran away before? Oh, you were wondrous! I can't tell lies anywhere near as convincingly as you.'

'Keep your voice down, Hetty!' said Miss Smith, clearly worried that Albert might hear, even though we were tucked inside the carriage. 'It's not an accomplishment I'm proud of, especially as I'm published by the Religious Tract Society. What sort of an example am I?'

'I think you're an *excellent* example,' I said. 'I will always love Mama most, and Peg was like a second mother, but I feel that you are very much a *third* mother to me, Miss Smith.'

'I'm honoured to hear that, Hetty,' she said.

I stared out at the great buildings all around, amazed that London was so enormous. I saw the most gigantic shops, their bright windows displaying beautiful dresses and hats and gloves and dainty shoes – enough to make every girl in the Foundling Hospital fit to greet the Queen.

'What's this astonishing place, Miss Smith? Is *this* Kensington?' I asked.

'It is indeed, Hetty. And that is Derry and Tom's department store,' she said. 'In fact it's where I purchased material for my own outfit.' She plucked at her black silk with her fingers.

'It's very beautiful,' I said. 'But why would you choose black when you could have any other colour – green or blue or crimson or purple or primrose?'

'Because this is a mourning outfit,' said Miss Smith.

'Oh dear! I am so sorry. Who are you mourning?'

'Well, originally I was mourning my fiancé, who died of typhoid. But that was many years ago, and now, if I am truthful, I struggle to remember very much about him. However, I've got used to wearing sombre clothes, and when I was younger they usefully deflected attention from other gentlemen.'

'You didn't wish to get engaged again?'

'No, I am quite content with writing and running

my home and trying to do good works,' said Miss Smith.

I pondered on this. I had always wanted to marry Jem, but now that I knew he'd spun the same stories to little Eliza, this didn't seem very likely. Perhaps I wouldn't get married, either. I would be quite content living with Mama.

I became so absorbed in picturing our future little house by the sea that I was startled when the carriage slowed and Miss Smith took my hand.

'We're here, dear.'

I bounced out of the carriage eagerly, staring up at the great red-brick house, which looked almost as big as the grand department store down the road. I loved all the patterns in the brickwork and the arches of the windows and the intricacies of the many chimneys and the snowy white steps leading up to the grand front door. I especially loved the twin marble lions that guarded those steps, sitting up on their haunches, their mouths open. Were they

smiling or growling? I patted their heads cautiously, and smiled when I saw that the door knocker was also in the shape of a lion.

'Would you like to knock, Hetty?' said Miss Smith.

'Yes indeed!' I said, reaching up. I banged the knocker as hard as I could, pretending the lion was roaring.

Miss Smith looked startled. 'Not quite so hard, Hetty!'

The door opened almost immediately and a very pretty lady peered out at us. She wore a cap and apron, but they were nothing like mine. Her cap was little, set on the back of her head, and her apron was so starchy white it looked brand new. My own was positively dingy by comparison, though it was clean on.

'How do you do? I am very pleased to meet you,' I said, bobbing her a little curtsy. We'd been taught to do that whenever a governor or visitor stopped to speak to us, and I was determined to show Miss Smith that I could behave beautifully when I wanted to. But

outside rules were confusing. The lady in the dazzling apron raised her eyebrows at me contemptuously and then looked enquiringly at Miss Smith.

'Merry Christmas,' Miss Smith said calmly. 'I'm Miss Sarah Smith and this is Miss Hetty Feather. We're here to join Mr and Mrs Rivers and their family for afternoon tea.'

'Certainly, madam. Please come in. May I take your bonnet?' said the maid – for this is clearly what she was. 'The master and mistress are expecting you. I will show you into the drawing room. Then I'll take the child to the servants' quarters, shall I?'

'No, no, Miss Hetty will accompany me,' said Miss Smith.

The maid looked me up and down, taking in my hideous uniform. She gave Miss Smith a look too. 'But she is a foundling child, madam,' she protested. 'If I let her into the drawing room, she might cause havoc.'

'Nonsense,' said Miss Smith. 'Miss Hetty has impeccable manners! Please lead the way.'

That told her! I smiled triumphantly at the maid. She crackled back at me starchily as she flounced down the hall. It was an amazing hall, tiled in such a bright turquoise blue it made me blink. There were embroidered hangings like great thick curtains, and a large rug patterned with leaves and blue flowers, as soft to walk on as any garden lawn. A very large turquoise bird with an enormous tail perched on a little side table by the stairs. I skirted it warily, wondering if it might attack me with its golden beak.

'It's not real, Hetty,' Miss Smith murmured. 'It's a stuffed peacock.'

'Why have they got a stuffed peacock?' I whispered.

'Why indeed,' she whispered back. 'Perhaps it's because Mr Rivers is artistic.'

The maid sniffed and led us up the thickly carpeted stairs. The servants here were very lucky. We foundling girls spent an hour a day scrubbing and polishing our own wooden stairs.

She flung open a door. 'Miss Smith and a child,' she announced.

I stood on the threshold, my mouth gaping. I had peeped into the boardroom at the hospital and marvelled at the gilt chairs and polished wood and larger-than-life-size portraits and sparkling chandelier – but that was a mere functional office compared to this room.

I felt as if I'd stepped into *The Arabian Nights*.

CHAPTER
FOUR

he walls were papered the blue of the evening sky, with violet birds swooping up and down and plump crimson roses bursting into flower. The carpet was a deeper midnight blue, and a very large white cat lay before the fire like a rug. I thought it must be stuffed like the peacock but, as I stared, it stretched lazily and shifted position. There were huge blue and white jars as big as me – and suddenly a boy's head poked out of one, making me start. I thought he must be some kind of mechanical doll, but he waggled his tongue at

me and I realized that he was real too. There was a big purple chesterfield sofa and a crimson chaise longue and a dozen or so chairs of differing sizes, all upholstered with tapestry pictures of flowers and animals. Assorted ornaments and trinket boxes were arranged on occasional tables about the room, and paintings covered the beautiful wallpaper.

I was particularly struck by the large portrait hanging above the fireplace of a beautiful lady with abundant black curls flowing past her sloping white shoulders. She was wearing a low-cut blue silk dress with lace and flounces. I'd admired Miss Smith's refined black silk, but I *longed* for a blue party frock just like this one. The lady lying on the chaise longue with a little dog was wearing blue too, and she had black hair, but she was older and much fatter, with a frowny face.

She was clearly Mrs Rivers, the lady of the house, and the tall man wearing a magnificent gold-embroidered waistcoat had to be Mr Rivers, and

the children must be little Riverses, all active and noisy, running around the room unchecked. Matron Bottomly would have been reaching for a cane, but Mr and Mrs Rivers didn't seem especially perturbed, though perhaps this was why the lady was frowning.

I didn't have time to count the children or distinguish one from the other, apart from the mischievous boy hiding in the jar and a baby kicking its feet in an elaborate cradle. There were too many other distractions. The ceilings were hung with green and blue and purple and red shiny paper chains that caught the light of the crystal chandelier. The fireplace was intricately woven with swathes of greenery tied into place with crimson satin ribbons, and a great witch's ball of mistletoe dangled from the chandelier.

A huge tree with great green branches stood in a tub in a corner of the room. It was decorated with candles and silver pine cones and glowing oranges and brown gingerbread men and glinting red glass

balls. Little silver paper packages were tied on with red ribbons – tiny parcels the size of Mama's shell house.

In spite of all the wonder I felt a sudden stab of sorrow, and turned my face in towards Miss Smith's arm to hide the tears brimming in my eyes.

'Merry Christmas, Mrs Rivers. It's very kind of you to invite me to join you for Christmas. I hope you don't mind my bringing an extra little guest with me,' said Miss Smith.

'Merry Christmas!' said the lady on the chaise longue. She didn't sound merry at all. 'Is this quaint child a *foundling*? Good heavens, whatever next! Look at her, she's quite overcome! Perhaps she'd be happier if Nurse took her off to the nursery?'

I gave a great snort. 'I'm not a baby,' I said, looking up.

There were one, two, *three* nurses advancing towards me from the shadows at the end of the room. One looked so stiff and stern and boot-faced

she seemed a prime candidate to be a matron at the Foundling Hospital. The second was small and stooped, and clearly ready for retirement. And the third was even smaller, about my height, and about my age too. There was something very familiar about her green eyes and the wild black hair escaping from her cap.

'Clover Moon!' I exclaimed.

'Hetty Feather!' she said. 'Oh, my!'

Clover had shared the splendid selection of cakes with me at the Northgate Tearooms. She was one of Miss Smith's destitute girls – though apparently not any more.

'You're a *nurse*?' I said.

'Well, a nurserymaid,' said Clover.

'And a very good one too, Mr Rivers tells me,' said Miss Smith. 'Now, Hetty, do you want Clover to take you off to the nursery or are you going to remember your manners and say how do you do to your hostess?'

I pulled myself together and approached the

grumpy lady on the chaise longue. Her dog lay curled up on her lap, a scrappy little thing like a hairy rat. It growled at me, obviously possessing the same nature as its mistress.

I dropped a curtsy. 'How do you do, Mrs Rivers. I am Miss Hetty Feather. I'm sorry I was a little overcome just now. It was simply because your room is so beautiful.'

She nodded complacently at my compliment.

'I'll wager it's very different from the Foundling Hospital, Miss Feather. How splendid that Miss Smith has brought you with her,' said Mr Rivers, beaming at me. 'Is it because you're the best behaved of all the foundlings?'

'I rather think it's because I am the *worst* behaved,' I said honestly.

'I do hope it is all right for me to bring Hetty, Edward,' said Miss Smith. 'She was rather woebegone because she had to go without her Christmas dinner, so I wanted to give her a little treat.'

'No dinner! Now there's a tragedy! Well, we shall be serving tea shortly, won't we, my dear?' he said, glancing at his wife. 'But meanwhile let's send Edie to ask Cook for a large turkey sandwich to keep you going. Poor Miss Feather, you're skin and bone as it is.'

Mrs Rivers didn't look too happy at this suggestion, especially when a plump little girl started clamouring for a turkey sandwich too, though her cream party dress was already bursting at the seams.

'Hush now, Miss Clarrie, you've already had two helpings of turkey for lunch,' the old nurse fussed. 'You'll give yourself a tummy ache. Why don't you show our little guest your new doll's house?'

Clarrie took my hand in her sticky one and led me over to a corner of the room. 'See here, isn't it splendid?' she said, showing me the most amazing house, so big she could almost squeeze inside herself. She opened the front with one flick of a catch and

showed me all the rooms inside, all fully furnished, with embroidered rugs on the floor and tiny gilt-framed pictures on the walls.

'Which room do you like best?' she asked.

I glanced from room to room. 'I like this one,' I said, pointing to the room that was full of miniature toys: a little bookcase with tiny leather-bound volumes, a spinning top, a dog on wheels, and a rocking horse with a long flowing tail. Mama's little house could have fitted in perfectly: a doll's house within a doll's house.

'Oh, I like the nursery too,' said Clarrie. 'But I like the bathroom even more. See, it's got a proper bath and, best of all' – she lowered her voice – 'it's got an actual lavatory – see!'

I *did* see. I picked it up to have a proper look.

'The chain doesn't actually pull, but you can pretend,' she said. 'Algie made me laugh and laugh because he sat all the dollies on it in turn!' She looked round. 'Algie? Where are you, Algie? Come

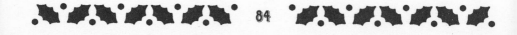

and show this girl how you play with the doll's house.'

I peered around the room for Algie. There was a big boy sprawled on a chair, his legs rather too long for it. He was playing with his pocket watch, an elaborate gold affair, making it swing backwards and forwards. He was far too old for silly doll's-house games. I could see a younger boy – at least, he was dressed in a boy's velvet suit, but he had a very girlish face and his long fair hair fell softly to his shoulders. I could imagine *him* playing with the doll's house.

'Is he Algie?' I asked.

Clarrie laughed scornfully. 'No, silly, that's Sebastian. Where's *Algie?*'

Mrs Rivers heard her. 'Algie? Oh dear, where is he? What mischief is he up to now? Nurse! Find Algie!'

The old nurse peered around short-sightedly. She sighed and took hold of Clover's shoulder, giving her

a little shake. 'You're meant to keep an eye on him!' she said in a thin, reedy voice.

The other nurse stood by indifferently, not getting involved. She just glanced at the tree occasionally. There was a girl kneeling in front of it, gazing up at the candles and the ornaments and the fairy doll fastened at the very top. She was pretty, with long dark hair and a deep red velvet dress with a white lace collar, but there was something odd about her. She was too silent, too absorbed, too still – until she suddenly lifted her hand, reaching for a candle.

'Stop that, Miss Beth!' said the boot-faced nurse, grabbing her hand.

Beth struggled, trying to free herself.

'No, no, naughty! The candle will burn you! It will hurt you and make you burst into flames!' said the nurse.

Beth understandably burst into tears.

'Stop that now, or you'll have to go to bed.'

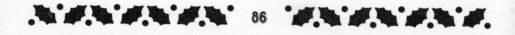

Clover gently led Beth away. 'You can look at the pretty tree as long as you want, but Nurse Budd is right – you mustn't touch.'

Beth sniffed and stared at the tree again, letting Clover wipe her eyes and nose. She kept wringing her hands as if they had a will of their own and she had to keep them under control.

Clover patted her on the shoulder and then went all round the room, looking for Algie behind the sofa and under the tables. Another Rivers girl joined her, helping. She wasn't as pretty as her younger sister by the tree, and the ribbon in her long hair had come undone, but she had a lively, alert expression. When she saw me staring, she smiled at me. She was wearing a green velvet dress, and she had three silver bangles on one thin wrist. That deep rich green would look wonderful with my hair, just as I'd imagined. I'd never owned any jewellery and would have given anything to have three silver bangles sliding up and down my arm, making little clinking sounds.

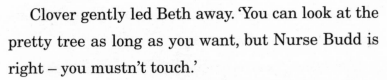

This girl looked very like the eldest boy, the one sprawled on the chair with the pocket watch, though he was taller than her. Could they be twins? Just now we had twin babies in the nursery at the Foundling Hospital, but they were sickly creatures, and Nurse Winterson said they were likely to die, poor little things. When I was a baby, I'd been expected to die too – I was fretful and light as a feather, and refused to take my milk. No wonder! I was pining for my mama.

Mr Rivers joined in the hunt for Algie, turning it into a game. He looked in ridiculous places, even the baby's crib, going, 'Algie, Algie, Algie!'

I don't know if he really knew where Algie was hiding. *I* knew. And from the way the eldest boy was acting, peering at his watch and whistling nonchalantly, I was pretty sure he knew too.

When Clover passed by, I nodded at her and then pointed to the largest blue and white jar.

'Ah!' she whispered, and nodded back. She ran over to the jar and peered inside.

'Clover Moon, whatever are you doing! He's not going to be in the wretched ginger jar, now, is he?' the nurse grumbled.

'Yes he is!' said Clover, giggling.

'Yes I am!' Algie announced, sticking his head up again. He looked so comical that everyone laughed, even the grumpy mother.

'Algernon Frederick Rivers, whatever are we going to do with you! How on earth did you get in that vase!' she said.

'I magicked my way in,' Algie announced, popping up and down.

'Stop it now – that vase is very precious. It was a wedding present from my own mama and papa,' said Mrs Rivers.

'Yes, magic yourself out again, young man,' said Mr Rivers.

Algie seemed to be trying, because his head revolved as he turned this way and that, but he made no progress whatsoever.

'Algie, get out of that vase at once,' Mrs Rivers commanded.

'I'm trying, Mama, I truly am,' said Algie. 'But I simply can't!'

'Nurse! Get him out!' she said.

The old nurse took hold of Algie's head and tugged. Luckily she wasn't strong enough to do him too much harm, but he shrieked even so.

'I think you'd better stop, Nurse, before the child's head comes right off,' said Miss Smith.

'Pardon me, ma'am, I'm simply trying to help,' she said huffily.

'How on earth did you get in there in the first place?' asked Miss Smith.

Algie said nothing, but I saw his eyes swivel towards the big boy with the watch lolling in the chair. 'I really can't say, but I do wish someone *could* get me out now, for I'm feeling very cramped!' he said.

The stuck-up maid, Edie, arrived back from the

kitchen with my sandwich arranged in four triangles on a blue patterned plate, with a little sprig of parsley on the top. It looked utterly delicious and my mouth watered, but I knew it would seem insensitive if I tucked in immediately, when Algie was still stuck in the ginger jar.

'Perhaps we might try greasing him out, seeing as he's so tightly stuck,' said Mr Rivers. 'Edie, you'd better run back to the kitchen and ask Cook for a tub of lard.'

'Absolutely not! Algie's wearing his best velvet suit. It will be ruined!' Mrs Rivers declared.

'Then there's nothing for it – we'll have to break the wretched jar,' said Mr Rivers.

'We can't do that! It's worth a small fortune. It's from some ancient Chinese dynasty, Papa told me,' said Mrs Rivers.

'Well, hard luck, old man,' said Mr Rivers, patting Algie's head. 'I'm afraid you'll simply have to live in the ginger jar for the rest of your days.'

Algie took him seriously and started sniffling.

'Cheer up, now. It's not so bad. We'll still feed you three times a day – and think what we'll save on clothing and boots! We'll be able to roll you into the nursery at night, and out again at breakfast time, so your routine won't be disrupted. And you'll find lessons with Miss Rayner a lot more pleasant because you won't be expected to do any writing or arithmetic,' said Mr Rivers.

'For shame, Edward!' said Miss Smith. 'The poor little lad's taking you seriously. Now let's think about this sensibly. If Algie got in, he must be able to get out.'

Mrs Rivers frowned at Miss Smith. She didn't seem to like Miss Smith taking command – or calling her husband by his Christian name.

'We are all doing our best to be sensible, Miss Smith,' she said. 'But I simply can't understand how Algie got into the jar in the first place. Did you take a great leap, child?'

'Yes, that's right, Mama,' said Algie valiantly, but his eyes were on the big boy again.

'I think someone lifted him in,' I said. I hadn't been able to resist the turkey sandwich after all and had taken such a mouthful that my suggestion was indistinct.

Oh, turkey is such a wondrous meat! When I lived in the country, I saw flocks of turkeys every market day. I had thought them very unappealing – all flappy red combs and wrinkly wattles and a great fan of feathers, and I found their constant *gobble-gobble-gobbling* very irritating. But now I was the one going *gobble-gobble-gobble* because the meat was so white and moist and tender, with no shuddery pieces of fat or gristle, and the butter was thick and the bread so soft and fresh.

I swallowed reluctantly and took a breath to repeat my suggestion, but the big boy pocketed his watch and stood up, stretching with lazy elegance. He strolled over to the ginger jar, slid his hands

down inside, seized hold of Algie under the armpits and pulled. He had to steer him this way and that because his shoulders wouldn't come out all at once, but he persevered, and eventually Algie popped right out like a cork from a bottle.

He gave a triumphant shout, unfortunately kicking his legs in their newfound freedom. His kid boot connected with the jar. It wobbled and then started to tilt. Mrs Rivers gave a sharp scream, though she stayed stuck on her chaise longue, her little dog yapping its head off. The big boy dropped Algie, hands reaching out to catch the vase, but Clover was there before him, clutching the slippery china with outstretched arms, staggering with the weight.

'Help her, Rupert! Well done, little Clover Moon!' said Mr Rivers, springing into action.

'My vase, my vase!' Mrs Rivers shrieked, but it was safe now, and Mr Rivers settled it firmly and then dragged Algie away.

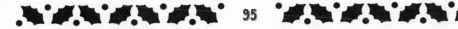 

'Steer clear of that vase in future, number three son!' he commanded.

'Yes indeed, Algie, you bad boy. If it wasn't Christmas I'd have you whipped,' said Mrs Rivers.

I started.

'I think our number *one* son helped him play Ali Baba,' said Mr Rivers, with a pretend frown at Rupert.

'Then he must be whipped too!' said Mrs Rivers.

I started again. I couldn't bear it when anyone got whipped at the hospital. I especially couldn't bear it if that someone was *me*.

Miss Smith patted my hand. 'Don't look so anxious, Hetty. I don't think Mrs Rivers is serious.'

'Indeed she is! I declare that each and every one of my children shall be soundly whipped, even the baby,' said Mr Rivers, miming the thwacks.

All the children laughed indulgently, apart from the strange girl staring at the Christmas tree.

The girl in green with the bangles came over to

me. 'Do they ever whip the children at the Foundling Hospital?' she asked.

I looked at her as if she was daft. 'Of course they do,' I said.

'But just for some truly terrible crime?' the girl persisted.

Mrs Rivers directed her frown at her daughter. 'Now then, Rose. It's not polite to ask such questions,' she said.

'I don't mind,' I said, gulping down the last of my sandwich and licking my fingers appreciatively. 'You can be whipped for anything at the hospital. My dear friend Polly was once whipped for telling our teacher she'd made a mistake – and she *had*. And Matron Bottomly once whipped me for insolence when I simply happened to roll my eyes when she said something ridiculous, though I can't really help it if my eyes express my feelings, can I?'

'Good Lord, is this true, Sarah?' Mr Rivers asked.

Miss Smith looked pained. 'I'm afraid it is,

though I am trying my hardest to make the regime less harsh.'

'It's terrible, children being whipped for such trivial things!' said Rose.

'*I've* been threatened with a whipping at school, and one of my chums has actually been given six of the best,' said Rupert.

'Yes, but you're all big boys, and fortunate ones at that. It's truly dreadful to beat little girls, especially *un*fortunate ones,' said Rose. 'Did they whip you today, Hetty Feather? Is that why you missed your Christmas lunch?' she asked.

'I didn't get whipped – I got locked in a foul room no bigger than a cupboard, and there are mice in there, rats even, and if they bite you they give you the plague!' I said, embellishing the truth a little.

'I would hate to be locked in, but I'd rather like the mice. I have a pet mouse called Montmorency. Would you like to meet him?' the fair-haired boy, Sebastian, asked.

'Don't you dare produce that wretched mouse, Sebastian!' said Mrs Rivers. 'Now, shall we change the subject? I'm sure the little foundling child doesn't want to dwell on her misfortunes.'

But this little foundling child could never resist an audience. I'd barely got started!

CHAPTER FIVE

 launched into a melodramatic account of life in the Foundling Hospital, from the moment the morning monitor woke us with her clanging bell to evening prayers and the chilly night in our narrow beds. Miss Smith fidgeted at first, trying to steer me into more general conversation, but when I elaborated on our one blanket even on the frostiest night, our unrelenting menu of porridge, stew and bread and cheese, and our endless dusting, scrubbing, laundering and darn-darn-darning, she scrabbled in her carpet bag for a small notebook and a silver pencil and started taking notes.

'I am more determined than ever to make as many changes as I can. I shall confront my fellow governors and *force* them to listen,' she declared.

'Good for you, dear Sarah!' said Mr Rivers, applauding her. 'And you must write a book on the subject! Tell the Religious Tract Society that I will illustrate it for no fee at all, because it's for such a worthy cause.'

'I think you're getting a little carried away, Edward,' said Mrs Rivers.

'Hetty herself will write that book one day,' said Miss Smith. 'You've been busily writing your memoirs, haven't you, dear?'

Rupert sniggered and muttered something, which made me furious.

Rose flushed too. 'Hold your tongue, Rupert. I think it quite wonderful that Hetty wants to write her own story,' she said passionately. 'So they teach you to write at the Foundling Hospital then?'

'Oh yes. I love writing,' I said. 'I knew my letters before I even went there. My foster brother Jem

taught me,' I said. 'I was brought up in the country and—'

'I don't think we need to hear your entire life story, my dear,' Mrs Rivers interrupted.

'But it's most interesting, Mama,' said Rose. 'So how many pages have you written so far, Hetty? Ten? Maybe twenty?'

'Twenty?' I exclaimed. 'I've written *hundreds* of pages. Miss Smith buys me special beautiful notebooks, don't you? And you're going to help me publish my memoirs when I'm a little older, aren't you, dear Miss Smith?'

'Then I will illustrate *your* book, Miss Feather,' said Mr Rivers, sweeping me a bow.

'Thank you so much for your offer, sir!' I said delightedly.

'Really, Edward, don't tease the child,' said Mrs Rivers. 'And if you don't mind my saying so, Miss Smith, it seems highly unlikely that anyone would publish the story of a foundling child. Good heavens,

a *foundling*! I know you mean well, but it's curious you should think fit to bring a foundling here.'

She kept saying the word, and each time it was like a slap across my face.

The girl gazing at the Christmas tree started repeating the word in a sing-song voice: '*Foundling, foundling, foundling!*'

'Now look what's happened! Beth is having one of her turns – I know it!' said Mrs Rivers.

'I'll take her away, madam,' said Nurse Budd.

But Clover darted across the room and snatched a gingerbread man from a branch of the tree. 'Look – this gingerbread man has fallen in love with the fairy because she's so pretty. Would you like to see him try to climb up to her, Miss Beth?' she said. She made him walk along the branch on his stubby little feet and then try to jump up onto the branch above. He didn't jump high enough and fell down.

'Oh dear. Shall we pick him up and help him?' she asked.

'Help him,' said Beth.

'There, well done, Clover Moon,' said Mr Rivers.

Nurse Budd and Mrs Rivers exchanged irritated glances but let Clover continue her game with the strange girl.

'What *is* a foundling though, Mama?' asked Algie, scrambling up onto the chaise longue beside her.

'Ssh! It's the child of a degenerate woman who has abandoned her baby,' Mrs Rivers whispered, but not quietly enough.

I wasn't exactly sure what 'degenerate' meant. It sounded very unpleasant. But I certainly knew the word 'abandoned'.

I rose up, quivering with fury, ready to spring to Mama's defence. 'That's not true!' I began, but Miss Smith tugged forcefully at my arm, practically wrenching it out of its socket.

'Quiet now, Hetty!' she commanded. 'You need to wash your hands after your sandwich. Clover, will you show us where to go, please?'

'Yes, Miss Smith,' said Clover. 'Come this way.'

I was whisked out of the room and down the landing above the turquoise hall to the stairs. The peacock glared up at me as I protested.

'I know you didn't want me to make a scene, but she was telling a huge great lie, Miss Smith!' I declared as I was hurried along.

'Mrs Rivers was mistaken about your circumstances, Hetty, but she wasn't telling lies. She was simply giving her son an explanation – though I agree that she was being remarkably insensitive and impolite,' said Miss Smith. 'However, we are guests in her house and we must behave accordingly.'

'I dare say you'd be furious if anyone said your mama had abandoned you!'

'I *wanted* my stepmama to abandon me,' said Clover. 'This way, Miss Smith.'

'I am sorry for you, Clover – but, you see, my mama wanted me terribly. She tried so hard to keep me, but she finally had to give me to the Foundling Hospital

or we'd have both starved. But then she came and worked there and watched over me, and it was so wonderful when I discovered that she was my real mother. We were so happy to share such a marvellous secret, and it was all so splendid until . . . until . . .' I found I was crying too hard to continue.

'Hetty's mother was sent away from the Foundling Hospital, but thank goodness I have managed to secure her a good post as a lady's maidservant, even without a reference,' said Miss Smith.

'I know, and I'm so grateful to you, Miss Smith, but I simply can't bear losing her all over again,' I sobbed.

'I understand, my dear. It's all so recent too. No wonder your feelings are in such turmoil. But you must try to control your temper, dear.'

'I don't think I can! Is it because I have red hair? Matron Bottomly calls me a red-haired child of Satan. Do you think if I cut it all off, it would make me meeker?' I asked.

'I'm afraid I don't think it would make any difference, dear.'

'Well, that's a relief, because I hated having my hair cut right down to my scalp when Peg left me there,' I said, patting my plaits.

'Careful – your hands are still sticky from the sandwich. Take her to wash them, Clover. I should wash your face in cold water too, Hetty, to calm yourself. I'll wait here,' said Miss Smith.

Clover led me into an amazing bathroom. The bath itself was snowy white, and it had dear little silver clawed feet.

'What fun! Do you pretend it's going to run away with you when you have a bath, Clover?' I asked.

'I don't bathe *here*!' she said. 'I'm the nurserymaid, one of the servants. I have a jug and a basin in my room up in the attic.' She turned on the washbasin tap and pressed a cake of violet soap into my hands.

'Oh, it smells so beautiful, just like the country-side! What's it like being a servant, Clover? I will

have to be one soon, though I don't want to be one at all. I hate scrubbing and sewing and having to curtsy to fine ladies,' I said, rubbing the soap round my hands vigorously.

'Now try blowing a soap bubble like this!' said Clover, demonstrating. 'I creep in here sometimes when the old nurse or Nurse Budd are cross with me, and cheer myself up by blowing rainbow bubbles. That's the way!'

'Are they often cross with you?'

'Quite a lot. But I don't mind. They don't hit me. Nurse Budd doesn't even raise her voice, but somehow she's the worst.'

'She's the stiff, boot-faced one, isn't she? I don't like her one bit. Or Mrs Rivers. She's horrible, though Mr Rivers seems very jolly,' I said, blowing a bubble almost as big as my head.

'Mr Rivers is wonderful,' said Clover, her green eyes shining. 'He's so kind to me. He encourages me to draw pictures for him, and then he praises them

no end. I know it's very silly, but sometimes I pretend that he is my pa. Those children are so lucky to have such a fine father.'

'I suppose it would be fun to have a father, but mothers are far more important,' I said. 'Do you know what, Clover – my mama sent me the most beautiful doll's house as a Christmas present.'

'What, like Miss Clarrie's?'

'Better!' I said, because Mama's little house couldn't have been more precious to me if it had had a ruby roof and diamond windows and an emerald door.

'All the children had a special Christmas gift. Mr Rivers is so generous. He dressed up as Father Christmas, with a red cloak and a false beard. He looked hilarious! He hid the gifts in the boot room in the basement, and then led all the children downstairs one by one, blindfold. Master Rupert protested that he was too old for such nonsense – he's got such a high opinion of himself now he's away at school. But I'm sure he's glad he went along with

the fun, because his Christmas present was that gold pocket watch, and he's very taken with it,' said Clover, sitting on the edge of the bath and swinging her legs.

'Did Rose get a gold pocket watch too?'

'No, she had those lovely silver bangles. Oh, they're so beautiful!' said Clover wistfully.

'Yes, I love those bangles too,' I said. 'What did Beth get?'

'She had a great big baby doll with a rocking cradle, but I don't think she liked it much. She wanted to play with her old doll instead, and made a fuss, so Nurse Budd took them both away, just to teach her a lesson. I hate the way Nurse Budd is so strict with her.'

'Anyone would think she was in training to be a matron! So what did the little ones get?'

'Master Sebastian got a set of great green leather books about animals. I glanced at a couple of pages and there were pictures of hideous creepy-crawly insects, but he seemed delighted with his present.

I only hope he doesn't want to start keeping insects as pets. That wretched mouse is bad enough – it's always escaping and then there's uproar,' said Clover. 'Master Algie got a rocking horse – a very splendid one with a long mane and tail – it's up in the nursery now because there's no room for it in the drawing room. Little baby Phoebe got a coral teething ring and a sturdy wooden dolly for when she's a little older. It was made by a very dear friend of mine,' said Clover proudly.

'Did you get a Christmas present too?' I asked, blowing more bubbles.

'Well, the mistress gives all the female servants lengths of material to be made into new dresses, and Mr Hodgson gets a gold sovereign and young Jack gets half a crown – but Mr Rivers gave Jack a fine knife and Mary-Jane, the scullery maid, a blue bead necklace. He gave me something special too!' Clover's pale face flushed with pride. 'He gave me my very own sketchbook and a set of pastel crayons!'

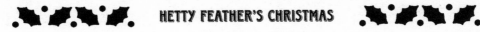 

'Girls, girls! Whatever are you doing in there?' Miss Smith called, knocking on the door. 'Are you actually having a bath, Hetty? Edie has just come to tell me that tea will be served shortly.'

I hurriedly took the plug out of the basin and let all the lovely soapy water escape. I took hold of a wondrously fluffy towel and gave my face a good wipe, because so many bubbles had burst there.

'My, you look very pink and well-scrubbed,' said Miss Smith when we came out of the bathroom. She caught hold of me by the shoulders. 'Have you calmed down, my dear? I hope you're going to be a good girl now.'

'Well, I'll try hard, Miss Smith,' I said earnestly. 'Is this tea just for the Rivers family, or do we get some too?'

'We certainly do,' she said.

'Do you think there might be more turkey sandwiches? Mine was so utterly delicious.'

'There will certainly be savouries,' said Miss Smith.

'And cake?'

 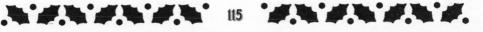

'I expect so.'

'Oh, there's cake all right!' said Clover. 'Cook made a Christmas cake and we all had a stir and made a wish.'

'Well, *I* wish that we all get a great big slice,' I said.

Oh, that Christmas tea! I have always had a very vivid imagination, but that tea was beyond my wildest dreams. There were small savoury pancakes filled with chicken in a creamy sauce, and tiny oyster patties, and little sausages wrapped up in bacon like a parcel. I didn't recognize any of these wondrous delicacies, but Miss Smith told me quietly what each one was as they were offered round by Edie and another maid and a gentleman in a tail coat.

I thought at first he must be the children's grand-papa, but he was a very important servant called a butler. He looked fierce, which made me nervous and I clumsily dropped my sausage onto the deep blue carpet. He saw me do it, but he simply kicked the sausage under a little table and gave me a secret wink.

The grown-ups had tea in delicate china cups, but the children had lemonade in big green glasses. Clover didn't get anything to eat or drink. She just stood at the side of the room with the other nurses watching us tuck in.

'Why isn't Clover getting any tea?' I hissed at Miss Smith.

'She will have hers later, down in the kitchen,' she said.

It was a relief to know she would be getting some tea, but I was sad that she had to wait. I was on my second helpings now, and considered casually walking past her with a pancake in my hand and thrusting it at her to keep her going, but Miss Smith tugged at my skirts when I stood up.

'Sit down, Hetty, and behave yourself. Don't you want your jelly?'

Jelly? I had thought the tea was simply the plates of savouries, but there was more, lots more – though Miss Smith confided that they'd probably all eaten

a vast Christmas lunch of turkey and roast potatoes and vegetables and then plum pudding and brandy butter and mince pies! She declared that she was still uncomfortably full of her Foundling Hospital luncheon, and shook her head when she was offered port jelly and cream, but I nodded eagerly. I also had several spoonfuls of something called a strawberry shape and, best of all, vanilla iced cream. I didn't realize how cold it would be and took a big bite that set my teeth juddering, but I soon learned to suck at the spoon and lick it like a little cat.

That *still* wasn't all! There was a Victoria sponge, choux buns with coffee filling, little lemon curd tarts, brandy snaps stuffed with cream, and a huge Christmas cake studded with almonds and cherries. I made it my mission to try a bit of each, and just about managed it. Then I drained my glass of lemonade and leaned against Miss Smith, utterly stuffed, my tummy tight as a drum.

'Well, Hetty dear, I think you're certainly well fed

now!' she said. 'I'd better take you home before you fall fast asleep.'

Mr Rivers clapped his hands as the maids started clearing all the dishes. 'Cracker time!' he said.

Algie gave a shriek. 'My favourite, Pa! Can I have mine first?' he begged.

'Oh well, you must definitely stay for a cracker, Hetty!' said Miss Smith.

I didn't know what she meant. At the Foundling Hospital we used that word when someone hit someone else extra hard, but I hardly thought Mr Rivers was going to punch little Algie, no matter how mischievous he'd been.

Mr Rivers went over to the large mahogany sideboard and brought out a big cardboard box full of brightly coloured paper twists, like giant wrapped bonbons. He handed them round, though he didn't seem to notice the servants. I wondered if *I'd* get one. Mrs Rivers gave a little warning cough when he approached me, but he ignored her and handed

me a pretty green cracker with a picture of a fairy stuck on it. I wanted to keep it pristine, but everyone paired up and pulled their crackers, breaking them in half with a snap and an actual crack.

This seemed a terrible shame. Beth clearly thought so too, because she gave a little scream every time a cracker was pulled, and clutched her own pink one to her chest, refusing to pull it with unsmiling Nurse Budd.

'Oh dear goodness, that child will be the death of me,' said Mrs Rivers. 'Why does she always have to be so contrary?'

Beth sat down beside the Christmas tree, bent protectively over her cracker, and started rocking it as if it was her baby. Clover sat down beside her and patted her shoulder.

'Leave the child alone, Clover – you're only encouraging her naughtiness,' Nurse Budd hissed.

'Can I keep my cracker too, Miss Smith?' I whispered.

'I think you might like to see what's inside,' she said. 'Shall we pull mine first?'

Reluctantly I pulled one end of her cracker. It burst open, and out flew a tiny pair of scissors – magical miniature scissors in the shape of a heron, its long beak forming the two blades.

'Oh! May I?' I picked them up and made the 'beak' open and close. 'How lovely! Do you think they really cut?'

Miss Smith rummaged around in her bag and found an old receipt. 'Try,' she said.

I snipped, and the receipt was instantly halved and then quartered.

'They work perfectly – and they're so sharp! We're only allowed the most horrible blunt scissors for sewing. I think the nurses fear we might stab each other. Well, actually, I wouldn't mind stabbing Sheila.'

'Hetty! I know you're only jesting, but even so, that's not a very Christian thing to say on the day of Jesus's birth,' said Miss Smith piously, but then she

smiled at me. 'I think you're hinting that you'd like my scissors.'

'It didn't even cross my mind,' I fibbed royally.

'I'll keep them safe in my bag for you. Now, don't you want to see what's in *your* cracker?'

I could see the point now and offered Miss Smith one end of my green cracker. A little silver object on a thin ribbon flew through the air and I caught it deftly.

'Oh, it's pretty. But what is it? It's not scissors. Is it jewellery of some kind?' I wondered.

'It's a whistle, dear. You blow into it and it makes a very satisfying noise.' Miss Smith demonstrated, and a little musical note sounded.

'Oh, I like it! Let me have a go!' I seized the whistle and blew as hard as I could. Too hard. The most amazing piercing blast startled everyone in the room into statues, hands over their ears.

'Hetty! Give me that whistle at once!' said Miss Smith, snatching it out of my mouth.

'Oh my Lord, she's trying to deafen us all!' said Mrs Rivers, plump hands clasping her ears.

'No, no, she's simply helping me attract everyone's attention,' said Mr Rivers. 'Now, children, we've had our Christmas tea and our Christmas crackers. What happens next?'

'The Christmas games!' they chorused gleefully.

CHAPTER SIX

hristmas games!' I echoed. I looked at Miss Smith pleadingly.

'Hetty, it's getting very late.' She consulted her watch. 'It's nearly your bedtime. Matron will be very angry with me.'

'Well, if she's already going to be very angry, does it really matter if she gets just a little bit angrier? There has to be a limit to how angry she can get. In fact, if we make her *incredibly* angry, then maybe she'll blow up and burst!' I said, picturing little pieces of Matron Bottomly all over the black and white tiles of the grand reception hall.

'You're a very bad child,' Miss Smith said severely, but her mouth twitched. 'No, we must take you back to the Foundling Hospital this minute.'

'But I *so* badly want to play a Christmas game. I've never played a Christmas game before. I don't even know what they are, but I'm sure they're splendid fun,' I said.

Miss Smith's expression softened. 'You have so little fun in your life, Hetty,' she said sadly. 'Very well. In for a penny, in for a pound. We will stay for the Christmas games, and hang the consequences.'

'I vote we play Snapdragon first!' Algie called. 'And you'll let me join in, won't you, Papa, because I'm a big boy now!'

'And I'm nearly as big and as brave as a boy, so *I* must play Snapdragon too,' said Clarrie.

'I would *quite* like to play Snapdragon, but I think Montmorency would be frightened,' said Sebastian quickly, stroking a little wriggling bump in his velvet jacket pocket. He had obviously liberated

him from his cage for his own Christmas treat.

'You all know I'm the best when it comes to Snapdragon,' said Rupert, taking off his jacket and rolling up his shirtsleeves.

'What utter nonsense! I'm much faster than you,' said Rose, rolling up her green velvet sleeves too. 'Beth, you can be very quick. I'm sure you could play.'

But Beth shook her head hard and stayed by the tree.

I nudged Miss Smith. 'Do tell me what Snap-dragon is!' I begged.

'You will see for yourself in a minute,' she said.

'And what's the matter with that Beth?' I whispered. 'Is she not quite right in the head, like Mad Jenny and Slow Freda and Stutter Mary at the Foundling Hospital?'

'Don't call those poor girls names, Hetty, it's not kind,' Miss Smith told me.

'But everyone calls them that, even the teachers and nurses,' I protested.

'That doesn't make it right, dear. But I don't think Beth is mad *or* slow. She's a very bright girl, but disturbed. I'm so pleased to see that Clover has the knack of handling her. She was very sweet and tactful with a similar little mite at my own Home for Destitute Girls.'

'Matron Bottomly frequently says *I* am disturbed, so why isn't she sweet and tactful with me?' I asked.

'I think you might try even the patience of a saint, dear Hetty,' said Miss Smith.

A rotund, red-faced woman came into the drawing room bearing a very large shallow bowl. It was filled with liquid, and she had to walk very carefully so that it didn't slop over the edge. She set it on a table and the children jostled for places around it. I went to peer at it too. It looked like a very watery pudding, with raisins and sultanas and cherries floating in the liquid. The butler turned off the lamps so that we were in darkness, apart from the flicker of one small candle.

'Are we all ready?' Mr Rivers asked. 'Then here comes the dragon!'

He touched the candle to the liquid in the bowl and it erupted into red and yellow flames.

'Fire!' I cried. 'I'll run for a bucket of water!'

'No, no, Hetty, this is the game. Mr Rivers has set the brandy in the bowl alight so that we can play Snapdragon,' Miss Smith assured me. 'We pretend that these are dragon's flames and we have to snatch the fruit from his fiery mouth.'

I thought she must be teasing me, but then I saw Rupert boldly thrust his hand into the flames to snatch a fistful of raisins. Everyone cheered as he tossed them proudly into his mouth. Rose elbowed her way past him and put her own hand into the fire, but then winced and pulled it back.

'Aha! Coward!' said Rupert triumphantly.

'I'm not a coward! It's my bangles – they get very hot,' she said, wriggling the beautiful silver bangles off her right wrist. 'Here – you hold them for me,'

she said, giving me all three.

Then she thrust her hand back in, and seized her own raisins with panache. While she was showing off to her brother, I couldn't help sliding one of the bangles onto my own wrist. I held my arm up to the light of the flames and the bangle slid down, shining and splendid.

'I'll take care of that, if you please!' said Nurse Budd, huffing and puffing. 'Really, Miss Rose – fancy trusting a foundling child with valuable jewellery!'

I felt my face go as hot as the flames and tried to pull off the bangle.

Rose's hand came over my wrist. 'Take no notice of Nurse Budd. You can keep it on for now, Hetty, and wear the other ones too,' she said fiercely.

The nurse gave a little snort and flounced over to Beth, who was whimpering. 'Right then, Miss Beth, what's troubling you now?' she demanded.

'The flames! The flames! It will hurt you! You mustn't touch!' she cried.

Nurse Budd sighed heavily, rolling her eyes. I felt angry on Beth's behalf. How was she supposed to tell the difference between candles and this strange Snapdragon game? Clover came and distracted her again, drawing her back towards the tree.

'I think they should dismiss that nasty nurse and let Clover look after Beth instead,' I whispered to Miss Smith.

'I agree wholeheartedly,' she whispered back. 'I might suggest as much to Mr Rivers at some future date. Now, are you going to take your turn at Snapdragon, Hetty?'

'No, thank you! It seems a very silly game to me,' I said.

I wasn't sure about the next game, either – Blind Man's Buff. Algie begged to be the first, so Mr Rivers tied a black silk scarf around his eyes.

'There! Can you see at all, Algie?' he asked.

'Not a peep,' he said.

Mr Rivers turned him round and round until

Algie was staggering dizzily and giggling. 'There now! Who will you find?' he said, letting his son go.

Algie marched about like a clockwork toy, his hands outstretched. He nearly stepped on the big white cat but she hissed a warning at him. Clarrie lay on the floor too, and when Algie got nearer she made mewing noises, trying to confuse him.

'It's Clarrie-cat!' Algie shouted triumphantly. 'And I'm a huge great dog and I'm going to bite her!'

He jumped on top of her and they tussled madly, Clarrie screaming and kicking. I looked anxiously at the two nurses. We always got horribly punished for fighting, even if it was only in play. But Nurse Budd simply tutted, and the old nurse remonstrated ineffectually, trying to pull them apart.

'Now, now, children,' said Mrs Rivers. 'You'll turn one of the tables over. Mind my ornaments!'

'Stop this rough-housing, you two,' said Mr Rivers. 'Clarrie, it's your turn now.'

Everyone had a turn at being the Blind Man,

even Miss Smith. She wandered around the room for several minutes, her black silk skirts rustling, but then she started moving in my direction. She put out her hands and felt my floppy cap and coarse stiff dress so it was obvious who I was – but when I shook my arm and the silver bangles jingled, she declared I must be Rose.

'No, silly Miss Smith, it's the foundling girl!' Algie yelled.

'My goodness, yes, it's Hetty!' said Miss Smith, laughing. 'Come now, Hetty, it's your turn.'

Mr Rivers blindfolded me and I didn't like it at all. I'd thought I'd be able to see a glimmer of light, but it was truly pitch black with the scarf over my eyes and I couldn't see a thing. Mr Rivers spun me round until I didn't know where I was. I didn't even know *who* I was. I wasn't *me* any more.

They weren't treating me like a real person. I was just the foundling girl here. At least everyone in the entire hospital knew I was Hetty Feather, famous

for my fiery nature and my sharp tongue and my quick wit.

I blundered around in my clumsy boots, unable to picture the room in my head. I walked straight into the sofa and stubbed my toes. People started laughing at me. I wanted to pull off the blindfold and stop playing the stupid game, but I gritted my teeth and carried on. I was very hot inside my brown uniform and I seemed to be getting hotter. Was it heat from the candles? I breathed in the green smell of woods from my country childhood. I had to be standing in front of the Christmas tree. I heard someone sniffing beside me. It must be Beth.

I didn't grab her. I'd seen how she hated to be held. I reached out very slowly and tentatively until I touched her soft velvet dress.

'Ah, the foundling girl's caught Beth!' Clarrie giggled. 'I bet she'll shriek – she always does.'

I could feel Beth trembling. 'Who can this be?' I

said. 'I don't think she's one of those naughty, noisy children.'

'Hetty!' said Miss Smith warningly, but I could hear Mr Rivers laughing.

'This person is wearing a beautiful dress,' I said. I moved my hand. 'And she has long silky hair. She's so still and silent. I think she must be . . . the fairy off the Christmas tree!' I took off the blindfold.

'Oh, she's so silly!' Algie chortled. 'Of course it's not the fairy! It's only Beth!'

'Bless the child!' said the old nurse.

'She's a bit simple, if you ask me,' said Nurse Budd.

But Beth was smiling at me, looking radiant.

'Well done, Hetty Feather,' said Mr Rivers. 'How clever of you! You are absolutely right. Beth is our own Christmas fairy.'

I glanced at Clover, wondering if she minded my being praised for handling Beth so cleverly, when

she did it all the time, but she was smiling too. And so was Rose. For a moment it didn't matter that she was the daughter of the house and Clover was a nurserymaid and I was a foundling. It was as if we were three friends together, in a secret club.

I gestured to the bangles to see if Rose wanted them back yet, but she shook her head.

'You keep them on for now. They suit you, Hetty,' she said softly.

'Is it Beth's turn now, Papa?' Clarrie asked.

'She'll only spoil it. She doesn't know how to play properly,' said Algie.

'We're going to change the game now,' said Mr Rivers. 'Who wants to play Charades?'

There was a huge hubbub and a clapping of hands. I didn't join in. The games had been a disappointment so far, though I'd have played a game of slapping each other with a wet fish if it meant I didn't have to return to the Foundling Hospital for another hour or two.

'Is Charades another silly game, Miss Smith?' I whispered.

'It's actually a favourite of mine, though I haven't played it for many years,' she said.

'Well, how fortunate that we invited you to share our Christmas tea, dear Sarah,' said Mr Rivers. 'Isn't that right, my dear?' He nodded at his wife.

Mrs Rivers forced a smile onto her face.

'I think you had better be captain of one team, Sarah,' said Mr Rivers. He looked at his wife again. 'Would you care to man the opposing team, my dear?'

Mrs Rivers looked appalled. 'I am feeling rather fatigued. I would sooner watch,' she said languidly.

'Then I shall be captain of the other team. Sarah, would you like to choose the first member of your team?' he asked.

'I choose Hetty,' she said at once.

'*Can* the foundling girl play, Papa?' asked Algie doubtfully.

'Of course she can, silly boy,' said Mr Rivers. 'A good choice, Sarah.'

'Can I be *your* good choice, Papa?' Algie said.

'Very well, Algie it is,' said Mr Rivers, though Algie seemed a liability, if you asked me.

Next Miss Smith chose Rose, while Mr Rivers chose Sebastian, the boy with the mouse. Sebastian went pink with pride.

Miss Smith hesitated, and then chose Beth.

'Fairy?' she mumbled, chin on her chest.

'Yes, you're our Christmas fairy,' said Miss Smith.

'And lastly I choose Rupert,' said Mr Rivers.

'Oh, Pa, I'm too old for childish games,' he drawled.

'Come along, son, you know perfectly well you can out-act us all. I want a winning team!' said Mr Rivers.

'Very well, then,' said Rupert. He sighed, but I could tell that he was really pleased to take part.

'Then I choose Clarrie to complete my girls' team,' said Miss Smith.

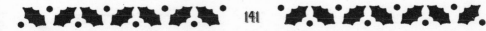 

But this suggestion didn't go down well.

'I don't want to be on your team,' Clarrie said fiercely. 'I want to be in the boys' team with Rupert and Algie and Sebastian.'

'But you're not a boy, Clarissa. Don't be tiresome,' said Mrs Rivers.

'I want to be on the winning team!' she insisted, and ran to her father.

'I would love you to be on my team, sweetheart, but Miss Smith would especially like you on her girls' team,' said Mr Rivers.

'Tell her to pick someone else,' said Clarrie, stamping her foot.

If any small foundling girl stamped her foot at a member of staff, she'd end up with a firm smacking, but the old nurse simply tutted and murmured, 'Now then, Miss Clarrie.'

Mr Rivers was equally patient with her. 'Who else can Miss Smith choose, Clarrie dear? I know your little sister Phoebe is highly intelligent and

forward for her age, but I don't think a girl yet to have her first birthday is quite ready for the challenge of Charades.'

I couldn't hold my tongue any longer. The answer seemed obvious.

'Can't Clover play?' I asked.

They looked shocked. Even Miss Smith seemed uncertain.

'No, Hetty, Clover is one of the servants,' she said quietly.

'But she's still a girl,' I said.

'Yes, she is,' said Rose. 'Of course Clover can play.'

'Oh, Rose, how typical of you,' Mrs Rivers snapped. 'You know perfectly well it's out of the question. The foundling child doesn't know any better, but you should surely understand the proprieties. Servants cannot join in family games!'

'But Clover was part of *my* family once, at my Home for Destitute Girls,' said Miss Smith.

'Quite right too,' said Mr Rivers. 'And now she

has joined *our* family, and of course she may join in the fun.'

The two nurses looked as if they'd each swallowed a very large dose of castor oil, but they couldn't really argue with him.

CHAPTER SEVEN

ow, my team, we must find a quiet corner to rehearse,' said Miss Smith.

'We can use my bedroom – it's much more private than the drawing room,' said Rose. 'Follow me.'

'I'll come too, Miss Rose, in case Miss Beth has one of her turns,' said Nurse Budd, springing into action.

'No thank you, Nurse Budd. Clover can look after her,' Rose said grandly.

I stared at her enviously. How wonderful to be able to tell a grown-up what to do!

Nurse Budd clearly didn't like it one bit, and

raised her eyebrows. 'Very well. I'm sure that's a good idea, Miss Rose,' she said sarcastically.

'Why is it called the drawing room?' I asked Rose. 'Is it where your father draws his pictures for Miss Smith's books?'

'No, he has his own studio upstairs for his painting and illustrating,' said Rose.

'The studio is right under the roof. It has great glass windows in the ceiling!' Clover whispered. 'I've had a peep, even though Nurse Budd said she'd have my guts for garters if I went wandering.'

'I'm sure Papa wouldn't mind,' said Rose. 'You peep all you want, Clover.'

We walked up the staircase together. Rose ran her hand along the polished banister. 'I once slid all the way down,' she said.

'I've always longed to do that at the Foundling Hospital!' I said. 'But I expect I'd get into terrible trouble if I did.'

'I expect you would, Hetty,' said Miss Smith.

'I got into trouble too,' said Rose. 'Which was very unfair, because Rupert, who's my twin, was forever sliding down and yet Mama just laughed at him and called him a pickle. She's never cross with *him*, especially now he's away at school most of the time. And *that's* unfair too. I'd give anything to go away to school, but I'm not allowed because I'm a girl. Life is so much better for boys.'

This was a conversation I could join in merrily.

'How I agree with you!' I said. 'The foundling boys lark about in the garden while we're all stuck indoors doing the scrubbing and sewing. And when we leave the hospital at fourteen, *they* get to be soldiers, while we have to be boring old servants – I can't imagine anything worse.'

Clover poked me in the back. 'There are lots of worse things,' she said. 'I like being a servant here.'

'Do you really, Clover?' asked Rose. 'I think it must be very difficult for you at times. Nurse is getting very crotchety now, and Nurse Budd is ghastly.'

'Now then, Rose,' said Miss Smith.

'But she is. She's here to help Beth – but she's far too fierce and strict with her. She's horrid, isn't she, Beth?' said Rose.

Beth bent her head and didn't answer. It all seemed so strange to me. These two girls had a grand life beyond my wildest dreams. They had beautiful clothes and dainty boots and wore their hair in long shining waves down to their waists. They had enormous amounts to eat and lived in a huge, wonderful house. They had their own mama with them all the time (though she wasn't anything like as lovely as mine!). Yet they didn't seem content. Rose was restless and *dis*contented, while Beth was troubled and withdrawn.

Rose's bedroom took my breath away. She had rose velvet curtains, rose-patterned wallpaper and a dark rose carpet. I imagined swinging my legs out of bed and feeling that soft carpet instead of cold, hard floorboards! The bed was wonderful too – wide enough to fit four foundlings, with an iron headboard

tied with pink satin sashes. The sheets were so white they dazzled the eye, and there were soft blankets, and a beautiful shawl embroidered with pinks and purples and deep crimsons as a coverlet.

On the windowsill Rose had lined up a collection of little china ornaments. Old dolls and stuffed animals sat in a row on top of her chest of drawers. There was a large bookcase crammed with enticing volumes. Best of all, she had her own little wooden desk with a pen and ink and a manuscript book on top.

'Oh, Rose, are you writing your memoirs?' I asked.

'It's supposed to be a sketchbook, but I'm mostly keeping a journal,' she said.

I longed to see what she'd written, but when I stroked the leather cover hopefully, she put her hand over mine.

'I'm afraid it's private,' she said, and quickly put the book inside her desk.

'I'd give anything to have my own desk where I could keep things private,' I said.

Rose flushed. 'I wish you had one too, Hetty,' she

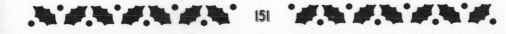

said. 'It makes me feel so bad when I think about the difference in our situations.'

'You're not bad – you're very, very good,' said Clover. She turned to me. 'Miss Rose gives me a little drawer in her desk where I can keep my special things, and she lends me her books.'

'I'm so glad to hear that,' said Miss Smith. 'Now, girls, we must plot our charade!'

'Please, Miss Smith, I don't know what a charade *is*,' I said.

'I don't either, miss,' said Clover.

'Don't look so worried! It's a simple acting game. We have to think of a word or phrase and then act it out, syllable by syllable, and then lastly we act the whole word, and the other team has to guess what it is.'

Clover and I stared at her blankly.

'Suppose our word was *Kensington* . . .' said Rose. 'We could have a first scene involving a man called *Ken*, and our second scene could be a little play about teaching a child to *sing*, and the third

scene could be a weightlifter in a circus lifting a *ton* weight.' She looked at us. I expect we still looked puzzled. 'A circus is a place where you see all kinds of performing animals and strange artistes.'

'I know. I've been to one. Twice,' I said proudly.

'Then we act out the whole word. So we could pretend to be cabmen discussing all the rides we've taken. I could say I've taken two ladies to *Kensington*, but I'll mention many alternative destinations too, so that it isn't too obvious. If the other team guess, they win. If they can't guess, then *we* win. Do you see?'

Clover clapped her hands. 'Oh yes! Then shall *Kensington* be our word, Miss Rose?'

'Well, they'll guess it at once, because that was the word that won *last* Christmas. We need a new word or phrase.'

We all thought carefully.

'Think, think, think!' Rose commanded.

'Oh Lordy, why can't I think of anything at all?' said Miss Smith. 'I'm supposed to be a writer!'

We started murmuring possible words aloud, trying to work out how we could act each syllable. Beth started murmuring too, quietly but distinctly. 'Foundling, foundling, foundling.'

'Ssh now, Beth, you'll offend Hetty,' said Rose.

I clapped my hands. 'I'm not in the least offended. Beth's come up with a brilliant word but we'll add another to make it harder!'

I suggested each scene excitedly and we hastily rehearsed them. The others were rather awkward and wooden, even Miss Smith, but I found it quite easy. I had done so much picturing in the past that acting was second nature to me.

Then the gong sounded downstairs and we returned to the drawing room. Mr Rivers and Rupert and Sebastian and Algie and Clarrie performed their charade first. They asked Mrs Rivers to move from her chaise longue. She protested, but Rupert managed to charm her into compliance. Sebastian took her place, looking limp and wan, while Algie

lay on the hearthrug, groaning dramatically and pretending to vomit. Mr Rivers was a doctor, dosing the boys. Then Clarrie came along with a mirror and the boys peered at their reflections and looked horrified, pointing to their cheeks and wailing.

We were all baffled until Clover whispered, 'It's *pock* marks! They've had smallpox and now it's left them scarred. There were folk down our alley who'd had the smallpox.'

In the second scene Algie was fully recovered. He seized a plate of cakes lying on the sideboard and started devouring them.

'No, no, Master Algie, you'll make yourself ill!' the old nurse protested.

'That's the point, Nurse! It's part of the charade. Go away!' Algie insisted.

He then mimed being sick again, and Mr Rivers declared that it must be something he ate. He emphasized the last word.

Ate? Pock and *ate*. It didn't make sense.

For the next scene the entire team seemed to be in a boat on a stormy sea. Algie enjoyed being sick for a third time, although both his mother and the old nurse declared that he must stop it at once. Mr Rivers took the first watch at the ship's wheel and Rupert took the second watch.

Aha! I nudged Clover and Rose and Miss Smith. (Beth wasn't concentrating any more – she'd turned her back on the performance and was looking at the Christmas tree again.)

'*Pock ate watch!*' I whispered.

The final scene confirmed it. Rupert pretended to wake up on the chaise longue. He conducted a running commentary as he got dressed, pulling on imaginary trousers and boots, sliding his arms into an imaginary shirt, doing up the buttons, shrugging on a waistcoat and then reaching for his . . .

'*Pocket watch!*' we chorused.

'I suppose *you* guessed, Rose,' said Rupert, looking annoyed.

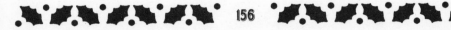

'No, it was a combination of Clover and Hetty,' said Miss Smith smugly. 'So, we have won the first round. And now it's our turn to act out our charade.'

I featured in every scene. I pretended that I was Sebastian and had a pet mouse called Montmorency. Then we all had to search the room until we *found* it. We had no luck until Beth the Fairy waved her wand (the little stick Algie had for his hoop). Beth loved this scene. Sebastian did too, and wanted to join in.

In the second scene I was a schoolmistress, while Rose and Beth and Clover were little girls playing skipping games. Miss Smith was a sport and pretended she was a little girl too, which was very funny. She actually lifted her skirts a little and jumped up and down. Mrs Rivers's face was a picture. I stood ringing a pretend bell, crying out, 'Ting-a-*ling* – playtime has ended. Come into the classroom this minute, girls!' while Rose's silver bangles set up their own jingling on my arm.

The third scene was highly inventive, even though I say so myself. All five of us were riding horses. This was quite hard to mime, especially as we're all female and Rose said we had to do it side-saddle.

'I know it's silly and uncomfortable, but that's the way girls are supposed to ride,' she said while we were rehearsing. 'I've only tried it once and I fell off almost straight away, which was very embarrassing, as my drawers were on display to everyone.'

'It would have been even more embarrassing if it was me, because foundling girls don't wear drawers,' I said.

'Girls, girls!' said Miss Smith. 'Persevere. Practice makes perfect!'

We were none of us perfect, and when we started galloping around the drawing room lopsided, our entire audience convulsed with laughter, boot-faced Nurse Budd included. Even Mrs Rivers's snappy little dog yapped in delight. Beth the Fairy was the only one who galloped with grace, twirling round and

round, being a bareback rider like Madame Adeline at the circus.

I took the lead, and Miss Smith warned that I was going too fast.

'Don't worry, Miss Smith, I have a splendidly steady *horse*,' I replied.

When we came to the fourth scene, it was our turn to mime illness, though not as graphically as Algie. Rose had said that she would play the doctor.

'You'll have to be a nurse,' I said. 'Ladies can't be doctors.'

'Oh yes they can!' Rose insisted. 'Elizabeth Garrett Anderson is a female physician and I admire her tremendously.'

'I do too. In fact, I had the great honour of meeting her once at a charity dinner,' said Miss Smith. 'Perhaps *you* might become a fine doctor one day, Rose.'

'Yes, and then you can cure all the little children who get the fever,' said Clover. She looked very sad. 'Like my sister Megs.'

Miss Smith put her arm round her. I felt a little left out.

'My brother Saul died of pneumonia and that was very sad too,' I said – though, to be truthful, for most of the time I hadn't cared a jot for poor Saul.

Clover and I were the patients, suffering from some unspecified illness, with Miss Smith playing our nurse. Beth the Fairy couldn't be persuaded to lie down and act sick too.

'I'm a fairy,' she insisted.

'You can be an angel, because I'm dying,' I said. 'Angels have even bigger wings than fairies, and they can work magic when they feel like it.'

I threw myself into the part of the sickest child, complaining that I was burning with fever and yet shivering too, with a terrible pain in the *pit* of my stomach. Dr Rose couldn't save me. I died very dramatically and was led up to Heaven by Angel Beth, flapping her wings protectively.

I meant it to be a very tragic scene, but the

audience seemed to think that it was another comedy and laughed a great deal.

When I announced the fifth scene, Mrs Rivers became restless.

'Surely four is enough! Your charade seems to have been going on all evening,' she said fretfully.

'Patience, my dear. I don't think any West End theatre could put on a better entertainment,' said Mr Rivers.

'And the fifth scene is very appropriate for today,' said Miss Smith. 'It was Hetty's idea again. She's very inventive.'

It was a Nativity scene. I had seen the Nativity tableau at the Foundling Hospital every Christmas, with Gideon suspended from the ceiling as the Angel Gabriel. Now we had Angel Beth, standing on a chair, her wings outspread. She kept astonishingly still throughout, though Nurse Budd insisted on standing behind her in case she toppled over, thereby ruining the effect.

Miss Smith was Joseph, with a chisel borrowed from the servants' quarters to show that he was a carpenter. I felt that Rose should be Mary, but she insisted she wanted to play a male part and was very happy wearing a silk scarf about her head like a turban and her father's fancy waistcoat as a splendid oriental king. Clover was a shepherd, with an old toy lamb of Clarrie's tucked under her arm. So *I* was Mary, my red hair hidden under a tea towel, holding a china baby doll as the infant Jesus.

I invited Sebastian and Algie and Clarrie to join us as stable livestock. They mooed and hee-hawed constantly, and I had to shout to make myself heard.

'It is *so* wonderful that you have come to worship my little newborn baby, who will one day be Lord of us *all*,' I said, very piously.

There were murmurs of appreciation from the doorway, where some of the servants had gathered to watch, and the old nurse actually dabbed her eyes, clearly moved. Nurse Budd's face stayed as

tightly buttoned as her boots.

'My goodness me – for acting and inventiveness your team have beaten us outright already, dear Sarah,' Mr Rivers declared.

'Nonsense, Pa. We'll guess their phrase from the final scene and then we'll be equals,' Rupert insisted.

'You'll never guess it!' said Rose, her chin up. 'You haven't got any idea, admit it!'

'Well, let us see,' said Miss Smith, discarding her Joseph garb. 'We will prepare for our sixth and final scene, when we say the full phrase.'

I actually thought they'd guess it immediately, as it seemed so obvious. However, we introduced as many five-syllable phrases as we could, simply to muddle them. The scene was set in my own horrible institution. Miss Smith was wondrously menacing as Matron Bottomly. Clover and I were foundlings. We tried to get Beth to be a foundling child too, but she insisted she was a fairy again and so she stood to one side, waving her wand. Sebastian and Algie and

Clarrie were happy to be extra foundling children, though their mother looked pained. *Matron Bottomly* (five syllables) was appalled when she discovered that Sebastian had a mouse and demanded to know its name. *Montmorency Mouse* has five syllables too. So has *History Lesson* and *Punishment Cupboard* and *Apron and Tippet* and *Bed without Supper*.

They kept guessing but they didn't get it! Well, Mr Rivers had a gleam in his eye, so perhaps he had an inkling, but he didn't say a word. Rupert kept trying, but we'd been acting so long he'd forgotten half the former scenes and couldn't work it out. He refused to give up until baby Phoebe started wailing.

'Oh my Lord, is that really the time?' said Mrs Rivers, squinting at the gold carriage clock. As if in answer, it struck ten times. 'Nurse, take the baby away for her feed. Sebastian, Algie and Clarrie, off you go too! Clover, put them to bed at once. Nurse Budd, take Beth.'

'My goodness, Hetty, I must take you back to the *Foundling Hospital*,' said Miss Smith.

Rupert groaned and hit his own head with the palm of his hand. 'Oh Lord, it was so obvious!' he said.

'So obvious you didn't get it!' said Rose triumphantly. 'We beat you, fair and square, two–nil! Clever Hetty!' She threw her arms around me and gave me a hug.

'Rose!' cried Mrs Rivers. 'Please remember your position! You mustn't embrace that child.'

Did she think I had fleas? Was she scared that I would somehow contaminate her? Rose hung onto me deliberately, ignoring her mother.

'Come, my dears,' said Miss Smith smoothly, gently detaching us. 'Perhaps you could fetch my coat and bonnet, Clover? Thank you so much for your wonderful hospitality, Mrs Rivers. It will be a Christmas Day to remember for both of us.'

Mrs Rivers looked disconcerted, not sure how to

take her speech. Mr Rivers jumped up and shook Miss Smith's hand fervently.

'My dear Sarah, it is always so good to see you. It's been a delight to meet you, Hetty,' he said. He shook my hand too. 'Rupert, say goodbye to Miss Smith and Miss Feather, sir!'

Rupert didn't bother to get up properly, simply waved a languid hand. The little children were being hustled away by the old nurse, but Sebastian dodged under her arm and came running back, smiling.

'I just wanted to tell you that Montmorency was delighted to be in your charade, Hetty,' he said. 'Would you care to stroke him?'

I wasn't too keen on mice. We had a plague of them in the Foundling Hospital, and sometimes a girl woke shrieking because a mouse had scampered over her face as she slept. However, I steeled myself and nodded. Sebastian reached into his pocket and brought out a small white mouse with pink eyes like beads.

'Oh, he's a very special mouse,' I said, and I stroked him carefully. His fur felt soft and warm. Perhaps if I was locked in the punishment cupboard again, I could catch a mouse and tame it and keep it tucked down my dress.

Beth came to say goodbye too, wresting herself free of the iron grip of Nurse Budd. 'Hetty, Hetty, Hetty!' she cried.

'Goodbye, Beth, Beth, Beth, my special Christmas fairy,' I said.

Miss Smith steered me out into the hall. Rose followed us while Clover handed Miss Smith her bonnet and coat and shawl. Miss Smith started binding me up in the shawl, and then stopped and pointed to my arm.

'Oh, my goodness! Here are your bangles, Rose. I almost *did* steal them, though I didn't mean to,' I said, wriggling them over my wrist.

'I would like you to have them,' said Rose. 'I insist!'

'No, Rose, you mustn't give away your silver

bangles, though it's a very kind thought,' said Miss Smith.

'I don't care for them in the slightest,' said Rose. 'They were a Christmas present from Mama and I don't care for her, either.'

'Now then, Miss Rose, that's silly. They're beautiful,' said Clover.

'I know what I'll do! There are three of them. Why don't we have one each!' said Rose. 'One for you, Hetty. One for you, Clover. And one for me. That's fair!'

'Rose, dear, that's very generous but it's totally out of the question,' said Miss Smith.

'It's surely the custom to give presents on Christmas Day!' cried Rose. 'You understand in your heart, Miss Smith. Please let me share my bangles with my friends.'

Clover and I stared at her. We couldn't *really* be her friends, for all she might wish it. Yet somehow, standing in the hallway under a dangling ball of mistletoe, anything seemed possible. Rose put one

bangle back on my wrist, gave the second to Clover and slipped the third onto her own arm.

'There!' she said, and she kissed us both on the cheek.

Miss Smith shook her head, but she didn't make me give the bangle back. She hurried me out of the door – and then we both stopped in surprise.

CHAPTER EIGHT

t was snowing! There was already a layer icing the pavement, and the two stone lions guarding the door had snow hats.

'Oh, how wonderful!' I cried, running down the steps and skidding in my ill-fitting boots.

'Careful!' said Miss Smith, catching me. 'Ah, there's Albert with the carriage. I'm sorry we've kept you waiting so long on this cold night.'

'I've had a few nips of my Christmas brandy, ma'am, and it's much appreciated. I also warmed up in the kitchen. Cook gave me a turkey supper fit

for a king. And puddings and cake until I was fit to bust,' he said.

'I'm fit to bust too and it's lovely,' I said, running in the crunchy snow, making footprints up and down.

I hadn't played in the snow since I lived in the country. We weren't allowed to at the Foundling Hospital. Once, when it was icy, I'd dared to slide on the way to chapel and Matron Bottomly had whipped me hard.

Now I ran full tilt, whirling around. My boot sole flapped and I tripped up, landing on my side in the moonlit snow. I was so happy I rolled over and over, kicking my legs.

'Hetty! Get up at once, child, you're getting soaking wet!' said Miss Smith, but she and Albert were laughing at me.

I was hauled into the carriage, and Miss Smith did her best to brush the snow off me and then wrapped me in the travelling rug. 'My goodness, you're freezing now,' she said, feeling my hand. Then

she held it and moved my arm, so that Rose's silver bangle slid up and down. 'I shouldn't have let you accept it,' she murmured.

'But you did, and it's mine now, and it's so beautiful!' I said.

'But what is Matron Bottomly going to say when she sees it?' said Miss Smith.

'I'll hide it,' I said quickly.

'Do you really think you'll be able to keep it hidden? Won't you be tempted to try it on once in a while? What will happen if one of the other girls finds it?' Miss Smith asked.

I sighed. 'She'll tell.'

'And then?'

'Matron Bottomly will confiscate it,' I said.

'I think I'd better look after the bangle for you for now. I'll bring it every time I take you out and you can wear it then. Will that do?' Miss Smith suggested.

'I suppose so,' I said.

'I don't want to spoil your joy in wearing it, dear.

I'm just being realistic,' she said.

'I know.' I was silent for a minute or so as the carriage drove quietly and all too quickly along the streets to the Foundling Hospital. 'Miss Smith, being realistic again, do you think I'm going to be in terrible trouble with Matron Bottomly because I've stayed out so late?'

Miss Smith sighed. 'I'm afraid so. I blame myself. But I promise I won't let her lock you up in that terrible punishment room. I shall insist that the Board of Governors forbid that practice forthwith.'

'Yes, please insist very determinedly!' I said.

'I shall do my best to concoct a convincing story to explain our extremely late return,' said Miss Smith.

'Will you say I've been abducted by brigands like you did before?' I asked.

'I'm not sure Matron Bottomly would believe it a second time,' she replied. 'Perhaps we could say that you fell over in the snow because of the deplorable

state of your boots, and you hurt yourself so badly I had to summon a doctor to examine you. You *did* fall in the snow, so it isn't exactly an untruth,' she said uncomfortably.

'Miss Smith, we aren't liars. We're *storytellers*,' I said, to make her feel better.

She laughed and put her arm round me. 'Do you think your outing was worth it, even if it has unfortunate consequences?' she asked.

'Oh, absolutely. I've had a wonderful time,' I assured her.

'I'm sorry Mrs Rivers wasn't very welcoming. She seems rather an unhappy woman.'

'She's not my idea of a mama at all. I feel sorry for all those Rivers children. *I've* got the most perfect, wonderful mother who loves me and cares for me and would give anything to be with me,' I said.

'That's very true, my dear,' said Miss Smith.

'I do miss her so,' I whispered.

I had a little secret cry in the darkness of the

carriage, but when we got to the Foundling Hospital, I was able to wipe my eyes with the rug. I took off my beautiful silver bangle and gave it to Miss Smith to put in her carpet bag. The scissors and whistle from the crackers were small enough for me to tuck down the side of my boot.

'I think I shall give the scissors to Eliza. She will love them. But I shall keep the whistle for myself. Maybe I'll creep up on Sheila when she's fast asleep and blow it in her ear!' I said.

'Don't you dare, you bad girl,' said Miss Smith. 'Come along then. We must steel ourselves to face Matron Bottomly. Courage, Hetty!'

'Yes, courage, Miss Smith!' I said.

'We will present a united front to the formidable Bottomly.'

She took my hand, and we trudged all the way up to the front door. The snow was thicker now, but I was filled with such a sense of foreboding that I didn't try to run or slide. We knocked timidly on

the great locked door. Nurse Winterson opened it, already in her nightgown, her hair tumbling past her shoulders. She looked much younger, almost like one of the girls.

'There you are, Hetty! I was beginning to think I should send for the constable to see if you'd been abducted,' she said, but she smiled to show she was joking.

'I'm so sorry, Nurse,' said Miss Smith. 'Tell me, is Matron Bottomly very agitated? I had high hopes that the bottle of sweet sherry I gave her would mellow her a little. I hope she shared it with all the staff . . .'

'I think Matron Bottomly finds it hard to share,' said Nurse Winterson. 'Come and see for yourself!'

She beckoned us along the corridor and up the long staircase towards Matron Bottomly's office. I held Miss Smith's hand tight. Nurse Winterson opened the door cautiously. There was Matron Bottomly at her desk, her cap awry, her chin on her

chest, her apron crumpled, her boots unbuttoned. She was snoring very loudly, but even in a deep sleep she still held a glass of sherry in one hand and the bottle in the other. It looked as if she'd drunk nearly all the contents herself.

'She nodded off straight after tea and she's been snoring ever since,' Nurse Winterson whispered. 'My, she'll have such a sore head when she wakes up! I'll tell her you were back well before bedtime, Hetty. She won't be any the wiser.'

'Hurray!' I said, but in the tiniest whisper.

I gave Miss Smith a big hug, returned her shawl, and thanked her so much for such a splendid Christmas outing. Then Nurse Winterson steered me along to the dormitory, her hand on my shoulder.

'Heavens, Hetty, your uniform feels soaking wet! Get into your nightgown immediately. Try not to wake any of the other girls,' she whispered.

Her hand seemed to be stuck there for a moment. 'Oh, this silly glue – I can't scrub it off!'

she murmured. 'I think you'll find Sheila has left a little surprise for you.'

'Oh no! Has she glued all my things together? Has she stuck something in my bed?' I whispered furiously.

'She actually felt very upset when you were taken away to the punishment room. She's been trying to make amends,' said Nurse Winterson. 'Goodnight now, Hetty.'

I was very wary all the same. Sheila was my worst enemy and I didn't trust her an inch. When, by the light of the moon, I had fumbled my way to my bed, I saw something small lying on my pillow. I picked it up.

It was my little house, mended.

It wasn't perfect any more, of course. The walls sloped, the windows were wonky and the roof had lost many of its shell tiles. But someone had done their best to glue it back together again, assembling each little broken shell and fragment of wood until it resembled a house again.

I glanced over at Sheila's bed. She'd tried to mend my house. *Our* house, Mama's and mine.

She was snoring, but I went and whispered in her ear anyway.

'Thank you, Sheila! Shall we be friends? Just for a bit?'

She murmured. I couldn't tell if she said yes or no. We'd have to wait and see.

I undressed quickly and got into bed, clutching my little house to my chest very carefully. I still loved it, even in its dilapidated state. After all, it wouldn't matter if our real house in the future was crooked and needed a new roof. We would be happy in a hovel, in a hut, in a hole in the ground, just so long as we could be together.

'Happy Christmas, Mama,' I whispered.

'*Happy Christmas, my own girl,*' she replied from inside my heart.

If you've enjoyed reading about Hetty's
friends Clover and Rose, look out for their
next story, *Rose Rivers*.

ABOUT THE AUTHOR

Jacqueline Wilson wrote her first novel when she was nine years old, and she has been writing ever since. She is now one of Britain's bestselling and most beloved children's authors. She has written over 100 books and is the creator of characters such as Tracy Beaker and Hetty Feather. More than forty million copies of her books have been sold.

As well as winning many awards for her books, Jacqueline is a former Children's Laureate, and in 2008 she was appointed a Dame for her services to children's literature.

Jacqueline is also a great reader, and has amassed over twenty thousand books, along with her famous collection of silver rings.

Find out more about Jacqueline and her books at www.jacquelinewilson.co.uk

ABOUT THE ILLUSTRATOR

Nick Sharratt has written and illustrated many
books for children and won numerous awards
for his picture books, including the Children's
Book Award and the Educational Writers' Award.
He has also enjoyed great success illustrating
Jacqueline Wilson's books. Nick lives in Brighton.

ALL THE TRIMMINGS

A VICTORIAN CHRISTMAS

Many of the Christmas traditions we have today come from the Victorian era, when Hetty Feather would have celebrated Christmas. Some of these traditions can be traced right back to Queen Victoria and her husband, Prince Albert, who had grown up in Germany. Some people think the huge success of a famous Victorian story – *A Christmas Carol*, by Charles Dickens – helped the traditions mentioned in that story to become very popular, and to be celebrated years and years on!

Before Queen Victoria, most people in the UK didn't have a Christmas tree. When she married

Prince Albert, a newspaper published a drawing of the royal family celebrating around a decorated tree – a tradition that Prince Albert knew from his childhood in Germany. More and more families decided to copy the idea for themselves, and soon every home had its own tree covered in fruit and sweets, gifts and candles.

Up till then, presents had traditionally been given at New Year, but this changed as Christmas became more important to the Victorians – and as presents became bigger! To begin with, people gave small gifts like sweets, nuts and handmade toys and trinkets, and these were hung on the tree itself. As presents became bigger, people started to wrap them and place them underneath the tree instead.

The first Christmas cards were invented by a Victorian named Henry Cole in 1843. He asked his friend John Horsley, an artist, to draw the picture for the front of the card: a family enjoying Christmas dinner together, and people helping the poor. Henry and John then sold the cards for a few pence each,

and within a few years the tradition of sending a card to family and friends at Christmas had taken off.

The famous Christmas cracker – a favourite of the Rivers family – is a Victorian invention too! Tom Smith, a sweetmaker, noticed parcels of sugared almonds wrapped in twists of paper when he visited Paris in 1848. They gave him the idea of the cracker: small packages full of sweets that would burst apart when pulled! Later, the sweets were replaced with paper hats, jokes and small gifts.

PRESENT-WRAPPING TIPS

❋ When you're choosing your wrapping paper, why not pick a different colour for each friend or family member, so their gifts are personalized? Or, if you're going to use the same wrapping paper for each person, try a different coloured ribbon for them all.

❋ If you don't like brightly coloured or glittery paper, plain brown paper and white string looks really elegant – and you can add a touch of colour with a holly leaf stuck on top.

❄ If you don't have any wrapping paper at all, see if you have any plain white drawing paper, and design your own Christmas pattern with coloured pencils, felt tips, glitter, and anything else you can find. Red and green are the most Christmassy colours, but you could try a multi-coloured rainbow theme too!

❄ Try personalizing your gift tags for each person with a joke or poem. You could even write a line from a song that makes you think of that person. Or you could decorate the tag with pictures of things that remind you of them, like their favourite foods, or symbols to represent their hobbies.

❄ Before you get started, make sure you have scissors and enough sticky tape for all the presents you're going to wrap – you don't want to run out halfway through! Cut off your bits of sticky tape and rest them loosely on the edge of the roll of tape, so you can grab them easily when you need them.

❄ Roll your wrapping paper out flat. Lay each present on it to check how much paper you need to cover it, before you start to cut. Remember the ends of the paper should overlap by a couple of centimetres, so that none of your present is left uncovered or sticking out!

❄ If you have several presents of different sizes for one person, try stacking them in a pile, biggest at the bottom and smallest at the top, in a sort of pyramid shape. Then use a long, wide ribbon to tie them all together, and tie a big bow at the top.

❄ If you have any wrapping paper left over, don't throw it away, even if you only have a few small scraps! Rip it up into tiny pieces and use it to stuff gift boxes or gift bags.

CHRISTMAS QUIZ

How much do you know about Christmas? Take this festive quiz to find out, and test your friends too.

1. It's traditional to exchange a Christmas kiss under which plant?

2. In the poem 'The Night Before Christmas', what sweet treats are the children dreaming of?

3. What item of a traditional Christmas dinner is set alight before being eaten?

4. Which saint is now known as Santa Claus or Father Christmas?

5. Who makes a special speech every Christmas, which was first broadcast over the radio, and is now shown on television too?

6. What must happen for it to be a 'white Christmas'?

7. Mince pies are now filled with fruit,
but what did they once contain?

8. Which of these is *not* one of Santa's reindeer:
Comet, Prancer, Klaxon, Blitzen?

9. What item is hidden inside a Christmas
pudding and is said to bring good luck
to whoever finds it in their piece?

10. In *The Little Match Girl*, the main character has a vision of a beautiful Christmas tree. Which author wrote this story?

11. Charles Dickens wrote the famous story *A Christmas Carol*. What is the name of the main character in that book?

12. How many sides does a snowflake have?

13. On the second day of Christmas, what did my true love give to me?

14. People usually place one of three things at the top of their Christmas tree. One is an angel; one is a fairy; what is the other?

15. On what date is it traditional to take your Christmas tree down, otherwise known as Twelfth Night?

16. In the seventeenth century, who banned Christmas in England for several years?

17. The tallest snowman in the world was built in which country?

18. Which two plants are often used as decorations at Christmas, are the title of a famous Christmas carol, and are also girls' names?

19. Name the three Wise Men.

20. Which famous novel starts with the line, 'Christmas won't be Christmas without any presents'? (Here's a clue – it's one of Jacqueline's favourites!)

FESTIVE GINGERBREAD STARS

People have been baking gingerbread for more than a thousand years, but the Victorians loved gingerbread as a special festive treat. You might want to ask an adult to help you to bake your very own gingerbread stars – wrap them as gifts for your friends, or thread them with ribbons to add a sweet touch to your Christmas tree!

FOR YOUR GINGERBREAD STARS:

☆ 350g plain flour, plus a bit extra for dusting

☆ 1 tsp bicarbonate of soda

☆ 2 tsp ground ginger

☆ 1 tsp ground cinnamon

☆ 125g butter

☆ 175g brown sugar

☆ 1 large egg

☆ 4 tbsp golden syrup

FOR THE DECORATIONS:

⭐ Icing in whatever colours you like!

WHAT TO DO:

⭐ Preheat the oven to 180°C/Gas Mark 4.

⭐ Line two baking trays with greaseproof paper.

⭐ Mix the flour, bicarbonate of soda, ginger, cinnamon and butter, and whizz in a food processor or rub it in with your fingers until you have a mixture that looks like breadcrumbs.

⭐ Stir in the sugar.

⭐ Beat the egg and golden syrup together and add to the mixture. Stir or whizz again until the mixture clumps together.

⭐ Tip the dough out onto a clean surface. Knead until smooth, wrap in clingfilm and leave to chill in the fridge for 15 minutes.

✫ Roll the dough out on a surface lightly
dusted with flour, so that it's about half
a centimetre thick.

✫ Using cutters, cut out star shapes in the dough.
Place carefully on the baking tray, leaving a gap
between them. If you want to thread a ribbon
through, make a small hole in one point of the star.

✫ Bake for 12–15 minutes, or until a light
golden brown. Leave on the tray for
10 minutes and then move to a wire rack
to finish cooling.

✫ When cooled, decorate your stars with
icing. Then wrap them in cellophane to make
a lovely gift, or thread with ribbons ready
to attach to your tree.

MAKE YOUR OWN DECORATIONS

Hetty is entranced by the beautiful Christmas tree
at the Rivers' house. Taking inspiration from the
following pages, why not have a go at creating some
wonderful decorations for your own tree.

Find some tracing paper, and trace around the
bauble shapes on the next few pages – or, if you
have a steady hand, see if you can simply copy
them onto a piece of card. Then cut them out
carefully, and pop a little hole at the top to attach
string so that you can hang your baubles up.

DRAW YOUR OWN CHRISTMAS CARD

1. Find a plain piece of stiff paper or thin card and fold it in half down the middle. Make sure it is turned to make a landscape card (as shown here).

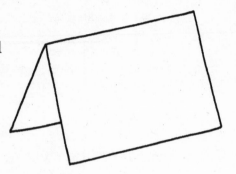

2. Draw the outline of a robin in the centre of the page.

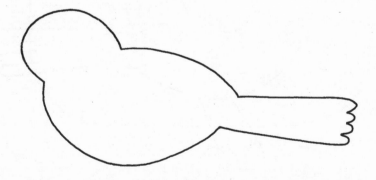

3. Add the wing and tail feathers.

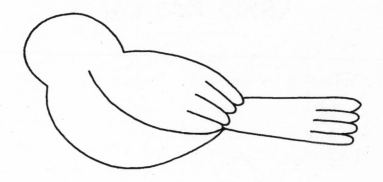

4. Then draw in the beak, eyes, legs and feet.

5. Give the robin a sprig of holly.

6. Colour your robin and holly. Make the holly berries shine by drawing white 'highlight' circles on them.

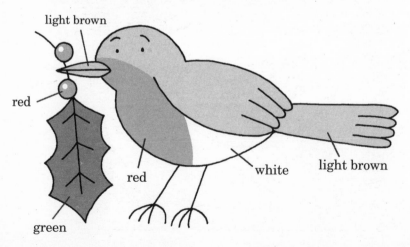

light brown

red

green

red

white

light brown

7. Finish your card by adding a decorative border.

Be as imaginitive as you like!

WRITE YOUR OWN
LIFE STORY . . . LIKE HETTY!

Hetty starts writing her memoirs after meeting
Miss Sarah Smith, who buys her a beautiful
scarlet, orange and gold notebook. She begins with
the day she was born – even though she can't
really remember that far back!

Why don't you try writing your life story so far?
If you need ideas, you could ask your parents,
grandparents or older siblings for help, as they
might tell you some interesting or funny stories
about you when you were very little.

You could write a new chapter for each year
of your life – or, if you have lived in different
places or attended different schools, you could
split your story into new parts for each
different time in your life so far.

If you find you've got lots and lots to say,
see if you can find a pretty notebook to
continue in, just like Hetty!

HOW TO DRAW HETTY FEATHER

At the Foundling Hospital, Hetty has to wear the same scratchy uniform day in and day out – even on Christmas Day! Follow the instructions to draw Hetty – then have a go at drawing yourself as a foundling, wearing the same uniform.

1. Start off by sketching the shape of her head, her skirt and her clasped hands.

2. Add Hetty's tippet, cap, sleeves and boots.

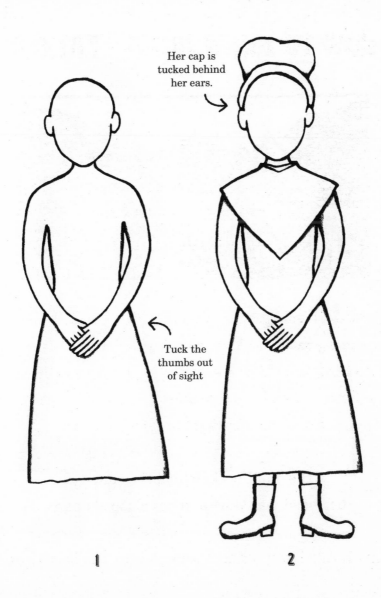

Her cap is
tucked behind
her ears.

Tuck the
thumbs out
of sight

1   2

See opposite for tips on how to draw Hetty's plaits!

3

4

3. Draw in her face, hair, apron and laces.

4. Colour your picture in. Hetty's hair is a wonderful bright red and her dress is brown.

HOW TO DRAW HETTY'S PLAITS:

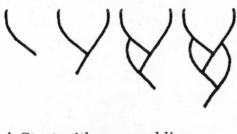

1. Start with a curved line.
2. Cross it with a line sloping the other way.
3. Add another curved line like the first.
4. Add another curved line like the second.
5. Repeat as many times as you want.
6. Finish your plait with a band or a bow, and a fan shape to show the loose hair at the bottom.

HAVE YOU READ HETTY FEATHER'S

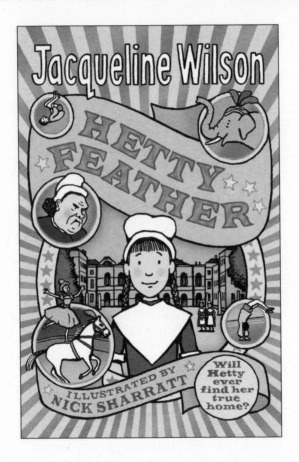

Victorian orphan Hetty is left as a baby at the Foundling Hospital – will she ever find a true home?

OTHER AMAZING ADVENTURES?

Hetty's time at the Foundling Hospital is at an end —
will life by the sea bring the happiness she seeks?

Following a tragedy, Hetty sets off to find her father –
might her sought-after home be with him?

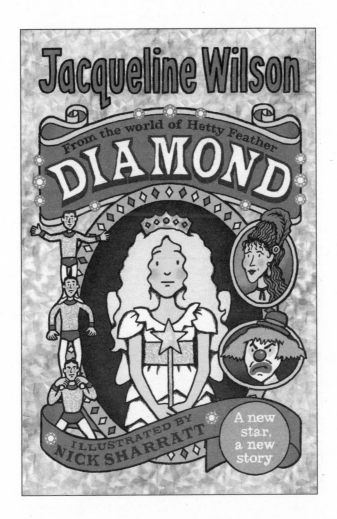

Jacqueline Wilson

From the world of Hetty Feather

DIAMOND

ILLUSTRATED BY
NICK SHARRATT

A new
star,
a new
story

Life at the circus is too much for Diamond to bear. Could
her beloved Emerald hold the key to a brighter future?

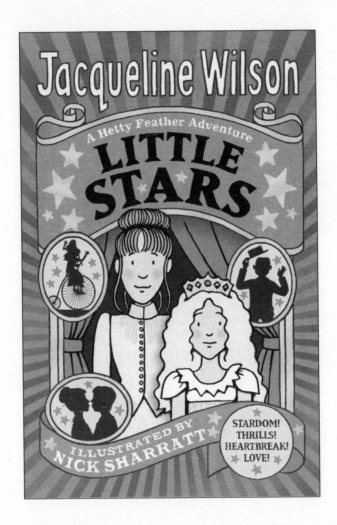

Jacqueline Wilson

A Hetty Feather Adventure

LITTLE STARS

ILLUSTRATED BY NICK SHARRATT

STARDOM!
THRILLS!
HEARTBREAK!
LOVE!

The bright lights of the music hall beckon – will
Diamond and Hetty become real stars?

Could leaving her home in a grimy
Victorian backstreet be the start of a
better life for Clover?

OPAL MEETS THE SUFFRAGETTES

Opal meets the suffragettes – and a boy who
might be her soulmate. But the First World War
changes everything . . .

A SECOND WORLD WAR STORY

Shirley misses home terribly when she's
evacuated to the countryside. Can she learn
to love her new life in the Red House?

VISIT JACQUELINE'S
FANTASTIC WEBSITE

There's a whole Jacqueline Wilson town to explore!
You can generate your own special username,
customize your online bedroom, test your knowledge
of Jacqueline's books with fun quizzes and puzzles,
and upload book reviews. There's lots of fun stuff
to discover, including competitions, book trailers,
and Jacqueline's scrapbook. And if you love writing,
visit the special storytelling area!

Plus, you can hear the latest news from
Jacqueline in her monthly diary, find out whether
she's doing events near you, read her fan-mail
replies, and chat to other fans on the
message boards!

www.jacquelinewilson.co.uk